Praise for
DEAD IS THE NEW BLACK

"A hit . . . grabbed me with the first page and didn't let go."
— Julie Kenner, author of
The Good Ghoul's Guide to Getting Even

"DEAD IS THE NEW BLACK equals *Veronica Mars* plus *Buffy the Vampire Slayer* multiplied by snarky sisters with psychic powers; secret cabals of vamps and werewolves; missing parental(s); and lots of mysteries yet unsolved. Nightshade is my kinda town . . . can't wait to hang there again ASAP!"
— Nancy Holder, author of *Pretty Little Devils*

"A fun ride from start to finish. Perez's smart and sassy style soars." — Mary E. Pearson, author of *The Adoration of Jenna Fox*

"Psy-gn me up for more of Daisy and her psychic sisters. Hot romances; coldhearted, soul-sucking vampires; and cheerleaders dragging roll-around coffins. What's not to love?"
— Gail Giles, author of *Dead Girls Don't Write Letters*

DEAD IS A STATE OF MIND

marlene perez

G RAPHIA

HOUGHTON MIFFLIN HARCOURT

Boston New York 2009

All rights reserved. Published in the United States by Graphia, an imprint
of Houghton Mifflin Harcourt Publishing Company, Boston, Massachusetts.

Requests for permission to make copies of any part of the work should be
submitted online at www.harcourt.com/contact or mailed to the following address:
Permissions Department, Houghton Mifflin Harcourt Publishing Company,
6277 Sea Harbor Drive, Orlando, Florida 32887-6777.

Graphia and the Graphia logo are registered trademarks of
Houghton Mifflin Harcourt Publishing Company.

www.graphiabooks.com

The text of this book is set in Adobe Jenson.

Library of Congress Cataloging-in-Publication Data
Perez, Marlene.
Dead is a state of mind/Marlene Perez.
p. cm.
Summary: When a gorgeous new student's prediction that a teacher
will be murdered comes true, seventeen-year-old Daisy is determined to solve the crime,
but when all signs point to the killer being a werewolf, she fears she is in over her head.
[1. Supernatural—Fiction. 2. Werewolves—Fiction. 3. Clairvoyance—Fiction.
4. Family life—Fiction. 5. High schools—Fiction. 6. Schools—Fiction.] I. Title.
PZ7.P4258Ddg 2009
[Fic]—dc22 2008000820
ISBN 978-0-547-33136-2

Printed in the United States of America
MP 10 9 8 7 6 5 4 3 2 1

To Michael. And no, I'm not playing Bejeweled instead of writing. Not at all.

DEAD IS A STATE OF MIND

CHAPTER ONE

I was running late. So late, in fact, that I didn't watch where I was going and slammed into someone walking out of the school office as I ran by.

"Ooph!" he said as my elbow jabbed into rock-hard abdominal muscles.

"I am so sorry!" I said. I'd almost knocked over a stranger. An extremely handsome stranger who stood there smiling at me, despite the fact that I'd almost flattened him in my hurry to get to chemistry class.

"Do not worry," he said with a heavy accent I couldn't place. "It is a pleasure to run into someone as beautiful as you on my first day."

He was dressed in a deep blue silk shirt, form-fitting black jeans, and boots. His spiky hair was really black, like someone had overturned an inkwell on his head. His long lashes framed incredible blue eyes.

"You're new here?" I said, stating the obvious. I knew

practically everybody at Nightshade High—and besides, it wasn't exactly swarming with gorgeous new students.

"I am Dukker Sherrad," he said, "but my friends call me Duke." He took my hand and held it longer than strictly necessary.

"Hi," I said.

He looked at me questioningly. I seemed to have forgotten my name as well as my manners.

"I'm Daisy Giordano," I finally said. I paused for a minute, waiting for recognition to set in, then felt like an idiot when my last name garnered only polite interest instead of the usual curiosity. You see, my mom is a psychic. She solves crimes all over the world using her powers. She wasn't exactly famous yet, but she'd been in the news plenty of times and I was getting used to people recognizing the name.

I blushed, amused at my overinflated sense of self-worth. "Welcome to Nightshade," I said.

Samantha Devereaux walked up as we stood there. She was blond, gorgeous, and the head cheerleader. She was also kind of a friend. Earlier in the school year, Sam had gone through a queen of the damned look, but that, thankfully, was over. She was wearing jeans I was sure would soon become all the rage and what looked like her boyfriend Sean's button-down shirt over a lacy camisole. It was outfits like this that earned her the nickname the Divine Devereaux.

I dropped Duke's hand. Quickly, but not quickly enough.

"Daisy, aren't you forgetting someone?" Samantha said pointedly. Remarks like this were why she was only kind of a friend. I thought *I* could be sarcastic, but I bowed before the master.

"What?" I was still staring into Duke's eyes, almost against my will.

"Ryan Mendez. Your boyfriend. He's waiting for you by your locker," she said.

Ryan. Oh my gosh! "I was supposed to meet him before class!" I said.

"I was hoping you would be available to show me around the school," Duke said.

"I've got to run," I said, "but this is Samantha Devereaux. I'll leave you in her capable hands."

As I left, Samantha said something to Duke I couldn't hear, and he laughed, dimples flashing. I felt a slight pang at leaving such a cutie behind, but another cutie waited for me.

I bolted to my locker, where Ryan was, as Samantha reported, waiting patiently.

"I'm so sorry!" I said. "I'm running late as usual."

Ryan leaned in for a quick kiss. "I don't mind waiting for you."

I smiled up at him. Maybe things between us were finally returning to normal. He'd been broody and distracted lately. He told me that he had been arguing with his dad a lot, which was odd since they had always been so close. I guessed it was because his dad could be strict at times—after all, he was the chief of police in Nightshade.

Broody or not, Ryan Mendez was the cutest boy in school (I pushed the memory of the gorgeous new guy out of my mind), played varsity in every sport the school had to offer, and was generally considered to be a catch by the girls at Nightshade High.

They also considered it a complete mystery that he wanted to be with me. I wasn't part of the popular crowd, although I'd been a cheerleader for about ten seconds back in the fall.

The warning bell rang, and we hurried to our classes. Ryan and I had P.E. together last period, but that was about it.

By fourth period everyone was gossiping about the new guy.

Penny Edwards was going full tilt when I walked into statistics class. Apparently, Duke was a foreign exchange student and was staying with her family, so she thought she was an expert on him. Who needed to call 4-1-1 when there was Penny?

"Duke Sherrad comes from a long line of gypsy fortune-tellers," she said importantly.

"Fortune-tellers?" I couldn't keep the incredulity from my voice.

"What's the matter, Daisy? The Giordanos can't handle a little competition?"

Did I mention that I'm psychic, too? But my abilities,

wonky at the best of times, don't hold a candle to my older sisters' talents. Rose's was mind reading and Poppy's was telekinesis. I can do both, just not very well.

Fortune-telling could mean that Duke had some sort of precognitive ability, if what Penny was saying was true, which was questionable. Penny talked first, asked questions later.

"Let's just say I'm a little skeptical," I said.

Penny barely disguised a sneer. "I think you're jealous," she said.

I opened my mouth, but the bell rang and Mr. Krayson started talking. "All right everybody, get out your books." He had an almost maniacal need for quiet in his classroom, and I wasn't going to test him.

A few minutes later, there was a knock at the door and Duke Sherrad came in. He handed a piece of paper to Mr. Krayson.

"I am very sorry to be late," Duke said. "I am not familiar with my classrooms as of yet."

"Please take a seat, Mr. Sherrad," Mr. Krayson said. He sounded positively affable, which was rare for him.

Penny gestured toward an empty seat near her, but Duke sat down next to me instead. Statistics was my least favorite subject and Mr. Krayson was my least favorite teacher, so the time crawled by. I spent the time counting the number of dirty looks Penny gave me. When class finally ended, I bolted out of the room.

"Daisy, please wait!"

I stopped and turned around. It was Duke. He hurried up to me, Penny at his heels.

"I had hoped you would show me to my next class," he said.

"I can show you," Penny said, but Duke sent me a pleading look. I took pity on him. Penny was a little much before lunch.

"What's your next class?" I said.

"Spanish," he said.

"I'm going there anyway," I said, ignoring Penny's fuming look. "I may as well show you."

"I am so grateful to you, Daizee," Duke said. His accent was even more noticeable now. He lifted my hand and pressed it to his lips just as we passed Ryan in the hallway.

I yanked my hand away and waved to Ryan. He waved back and gave me a quizzical look but kept going. He had Mr. Krayson next, so I knew he didn't have time to slow down, not without getting a tardy slip and a ten-minute lecture on punctuality.

In Spanish class, Duke once again managed to find a seat near me. All he had to do was smile charmingly at Alyssa and she gave it up right away. Her seat, I mean, although gauging from the look in her eyes, she may have had a few other things in mind.

I finally shook Duke off after Spanish class. I couldn't put my finger on why, but he was making me uneasy.

I dumped my books in my locker, and as I reached in to grab my lunch money, arms twined around my waist and pulled me against a hard body.

"Ryan, you scared the heck out of me!" I said.

"Who else would be grabbing you?" he said. "Is there something you want to tell me?"

"Of course not," I said. "I just wasn't expecting it."

He drew me closer and gave me a lingering kiss. "So who's your new admirer?" He said it casually, but I could feel his body tense.

"You mean Duke Sherrad?" I laughed like it was no big deal. Gorgeous or not, Duke didn't mean anything to me. Ryan did.

"I saw him kissing your hand in the hallway," Ryan said. His green eyes were intense.

"It was nothing," I said. I didn't mention anything about Duke sitting next to me in every class we shared.

"Good," he said. He leaned against the wall, pulled me close, and kissed me again. Several minutes later, he took a deep breath and said, "Are you hungry?"

"Starving," I admitted. "But by now there's probably nothing left at the cafeteria but cold tater tots."

"I planned ahead," he said, smiling triumphantly. He produced a picnic basket and tablecloth. "I thought we could have a picnic."

We went outside to find a shady spot on the lawn. A gaggle of girls had gathered around Duke Sherrad. Penny elbowed Alyssa when she tried to sit next to him.

Even Samantha was in his group. "Daisy, why don't you and Ryan come over here? Duke is telling our fortunes."

"Ryan packed a picnic," I said. "Thanks anyway."

"How about that spot over there?" I said. I pointed to a spot as far away from Duke as possible without actually leaving the school grounds.

While Ryan unpacked the food, I stared at Duke. A fortune-teller, huh?

"You okay?" Ryan asked. He handed me a huge deli sandwich from Slim's Diner. My favorite restaurant.

"Fine," I said. I took a bite of my sandwich. "This was so sweet of you."

"I wanted to do something to make up for the way I've been acting lately," he said. "I know I haven't been the easiest guy to be around."

I took his hand. "It's okay."

"It isn't, but thanks for bearing with me," he said.

"Ryan, about prom—"

A piercing scream interrupted my words. Ryan and I leaped to our feet and ran toward the sound. Just another typical day at Nightshade High.

CHAPTER TWO

"What's wrong?" I asked, panting from the dash across the lawn.

Penny looked at me scornfully. "Nothing is wrong," she said.

"Just the best news ever!" Alyssa screeched. "Duke predicted that I would meet someone tall, dark, and handsome in the near future!"

"Did he tell you that you were taking a long journey, too?" I muttered. Both "predictions" might as well be in the phony fortune-tellers' handbook. Not exactly confidence inspiring.

Penny looked sour at the mention of someone else getting a tall, dark, and handsome stranger but then brightened. "He told me that I'd have a mysterious encounter. And it's already come true. Last night, I was walking by the mortuary when I saw a light."

"Did you move toward it?"

"What?" she said. She didn't get it.

I changed the subject. "What's so mysterious about a light at the mortuary? It was probably just Mr. Bone or Nicholas working late." I assumed that it was actually a meeting of the Nightshade City Council, a secret group made up of members of the thirteen founding families of Nightshade, but that was something I wasn't going to share with Penny.

"I looked in a window. The light was just hovering there in midair. And then the wailing and banging began."

Penny was prone to exaggeration, but I still decided I'd ask Rose about it after school. Rose was my oldest sister and was dating Nicholas Bone, whose family owned Mort's Mortuary.

"Daizee," Duke said. "I looked for you after Spanish class."

"I had lunch plans," I said. "Ryan, this is Duke Sherrad. Duke, this is Ryan Mendez."

"Her boyfriend," Ryan added, smiling pleasantly, if you call baring your teeth smiling. He took my hand and pulled me to his side, but Duke ignored Ryan's show of possessiveness.

"I would be happy to give you a private reading," he said.

Ryan glared but didn't say anything.

"Uh, maybe some other time," I said.

The testosterone was thick in the air. Just as I was beginning to fear a fight, Mr. Davis, the journalism teacher, approached the group.

"Samantha," he said, "I hope you'll be trying out for the play next week."

She beamed at him. "Yes, Mr. Davis. I will."

"Me, too!" Alyssa piped in, batting her eyelashes. Girls were always flirting with Mr. Davis. He was one of the youngest teachers at school, and he helped with the play every year.

"Have you met Duke yet?" Penny asked. "He'd be a perfect leading man."

Mr. Davis's smile faded and his jaw dropped when he saw the new student. I wondered why. Was he scared of a little competition for the girls' attention?

"I am afraid I'm not much of an actor," Duke said. "How do you say it? My accent is too thick for your American audiences to understand."

I had had enough of the Duke Sherrad Fan Club meeting, so Ryan and I went back to our picnic.

"So, Duke is in some of your classes?" Ryan asked casually, a few minutes later.

"Two so far," I admitted. "Why?"

"Just curious," he said.

I changed the subject. I didn't want to talk about Duke. Something about him made me uncomfortable. I wasn't used to all that attention from someone I didn't know.

"Hey, Side Effects May Vary is playing at the Black Opal in a couple of weeks," I said. "Do you want to get tickets? Nicholas and Rose are going."

"Sounds great," Ryan said. "How is Rose doing, by the way? I haven't seen her in a while."

My sister Rose was in college at UC Nightshade, but she

still lived at home. Lately, all the time she wasn't studying she was spending with Nicholas. Things were getting pretty hot and heavy with those two.

"She's fine, but I don't know how she does it," I admitted.

"What do you mean?"

I looked over at him, startled by a strange note in his voice. "I'm just not sure I could be so, so . . . cool with the whole werewolf thing."

"Maybe she loves him." His voice sounded grim. "If you love someone, it shouldn't matter."

"Of course Rose loves him," I said, "but that doesn't make it any easier. She's not a shifter."

What I really worried about was my sister getting her heart broken again. Nicholas had already dumped her once, when he first found out he was a werewolf.

The bell rang, and Ryan walked me to class.

"I'll see you later in P.E., okay?" he said. He squeezed my hand and then jogged off toward his next class.

While I sat in American government, I tried to pay attention, but my mind kept drifting back to my conversation with Ryan. He had been distant lately and had seemed almost angry when we talked about Rose and Nicholas. Ryan and I had been friends forever, but our relationship, at least our romantic one, was so new. Was the romance already dead?

A voice interrupted my thoughts. "The prom committee is looking for more volunteers," Mrs. Lambert said.

Samantha nudged me with her foot, but I ignored her.

She nudged me again. Samantha was one of the bossiest people I knew, but she meant well. A little participation wouldn't kill me.

I sighed and raised my hand.

"Daisy," Mrs. Lambert said. "Excellent."

When dismissal bell rang, I hurried to my locker. On the way I spotted Duke deep in conversation with Mr. Davis. I wondered what he could have to say to the journalism teacher. Duke didn't seem like the school newspaper type, unless he was offering to write horoscopes.

"Daisy! Wait up," a voice called out. Samantha jogged up to me.

"What's up?"

"Do you want to help us make prom posters after school?" she asked.

"Sure," I said. After all, I had volunteered. Lots of my old cheerleader pals were on the prom committee, so it would be nice to catch up with them. I didn't see them as often now that I'd quit cheerleading.

Samantha led the way to the gym, where the prom committee members sat at long tables, armed with sparkly paint and poster board.

Rachel rushed up to me. "Hi, Daisy! It's great that you're helping us." She gave me a hug. "Anytime you want back in the squad, you just holler."

I smiled and nodded but avoided telling her that I'd rather walk over broken glass than get back into a skimpy cheerleading uniform. Last time it had only been because the cheerleaders seemed to be in danger and I thought I could help.

Samantha and I sat down and got to work.

"Don't forget to include the location, the time, and the cost of tickets," Samantha said, handing me a blank poster and some glue.

"Oh, yeah," I said. "Where is prom going to be this year, anyway?"

Penny rolled her eyes. "The Wilder mansion, duh! We only chose the place about a year ago."

"Well, that was before Daisy joined the committee," Sam said judiciously. "The good places go fast," she told me.

The Wilder mansion was the oldest building in town, and nobody had lived there for many years. When I was small, it had been a crumbling old building full of dust and bats. But Mrs. Wilder had spent the last two years restoring it to its former glory.

"How does it look in there?" I asked Sam. "It was in rough shape for a long time."

"Oh, it's amazing," she gushed. "The place is practically dripping with gold. That family is loaded. There's a wing with their private residence, and another wing where there's a ballroom and a little restaurant where they serve afternoon tea."

"Sounds fabulous," I said.

Samantha sprinkled some glitter on her poster. "Maybe we can double," she said.

"Double where?" I asked. Samantha dated Sean Walsh, who was the quarterback of the football team, star catcher on the baseball team, and all-round big man on campus. He also lived next door to me.

"A double date for the prom," she said.

Our last double date hadn't gone so well. I'd found an unconscious girl in the bathroom of the Black Opal, an all-ages club.

"Ryan hasn't asked me yet." I glanced at Penny, who was listening in with her mouth open.

"Well, he'd better not wait too long," Samantha said. "I hear there's another interested party."

"Who?" I asked, loudly. Penny's ears perked up again. "Who?" I repeated, this time in a lower voice.

Samantha glanced at Penny and then leaned in so we wouldn't be overheard. "I hear Duke Sherrad is smitten with you."

"I was over guys like Duke Sherrad when I was twelve," I said.

Samantha looked at me shrewdly. I don't know why I mentioned that age. The age I was when my dad left us. "Well, all I'm saying is that Ryan had better hurry. You can't wait forever."

"We don't even have the prom posters up yet," I pointed out. "He probably hasn't even thought about it. When did Sean ask you?"

"Last month," she said.

Sean *was* whipped, but I was starting to worry that Ryan wasn't planning on asking me.

"Does everyone else on the squad have dates?" I gestured toward Penny and Rachel, who were sitting at a table near us.

"Not Penny, but Rachel is going with Z," she said. Z was short for Adam Zeigler. My sister Poppy had dated him briefly, but they hadn't been seeing each other lately. Poppy had been having a date drought during her senior year.

I didn't want to be in any category with Penny, but dateless for prom was definitely the category to avoid.

"What about everyone else?" I nodded toward the row of cheerleaders.

She shrugged. "The popular girls get asked early."

I raised an eyebrow and looked at her solemnly.

"I mean—everyone knows Ryan will—oh, you know what I mean," she said as I slowly cracked a grin.

I had to admit that I had fun with Samantha. We'd been best friends until middle school, then enemies, and now we were working our way back toward friends again. We hadn't made it all the way back to trusting each other yet. Sam had her secrets, and I had mine.

And speaking of secrets . . .

"How are your parents?" I asked. The last time I'd been at the Devereaux house I'd found a secret stack of overdue bills, which was odd, since the Devereauxs were one of the wealthiest families in town. Or at least they had been.

"They're traveling again. Mom's in San Francisco, and Daddy's on tour."

Before my father disappeared, he and Samantha's father had been colleagues at the local college, UC Nightshade. Her father made a bundle off a book he wrote using much of the research he had done with my father. Of course, Rafe Giordano wasn't around to complain about the unfairness of it all.

An hour later, we were finished with the glitter, glue, and smelly markers.

"Do you want a ride home?" Samantha asked. "I'm heading that way anyway. I'm going to hang out at Sean's house and wait for him to get out of baseball."

"Sure, thanks." We headed for her car, a newer-model BMW convertible.

I was curious why Samantha would want to hang out at Sean's house, with all his little brothers and sisters running around, when she could be relaxing in her giant Jacuzzi in the privacy of her own home. Was Samantha lonely all by herself in that big house?

"Do you want to help hang the posters Thursday after school?" she asked.

"Sure." The sooner the posters were up, then maybe the sooner Ryan would take the hint.

"Hey, do you want to hang out at my house until the guys are through with baseball practice?" I asked as we pulled onto my street.

"Maybe another time," she said. "I promised Katie that I'd help her make cookies." Katie was one of Sean's little sisters.

"See you later." Samantha parked the car, and I headed to my house. She headed next door.

I threw my backpack down on the hallway table and went to the kitchen to make a snack. Rose sat at the counter, her nose in a book. She tended to zone everyone out when she was studying. I had to say hello twice before she looked up.

"Oh, hey, Daisy," she said. "I'm glad you're home. What are you making tonight? I invited Nicholas over for dinner."

Since Mom always worked late, I did almost all the cooking in our house. What did werewolves eat? Could I use garlic? If not, that left out half of Grandma Giordano's recipes. Oh, wait. Vampires were repelled by garlic. It took silver bullets for werewolves.

After a moment of consideration, I said, "I'll make fettuccini Bolognese. Werewolves like meat, right?"

"*Nicholas*," she said firmly, "likes everything. Whatever you make is fine. We haven't had fettuccini in ages. But do you have time?"

"If you run to the grocery store," I said, "I'll make some

minestrone to start, too. Mom loves that. I have everything I need for the soup."

As I handed Rose the grocery list, Poppy appeared in the doorway.

"Need any help with dinner?" she asked. "I'm starving!"

"Can you chop the vegetables?"

Poppy didn't answer, but the fridge door opened and a parade of veggies floated onto the cutting board. She winked at me. "You should practice your powers more often. You'd be the fastest chef ever."

She had a point. The minestrone was simmering on the stove just minutes after Rose left. By the time she got back with the ground pork and ground veal, I had the sauce made and everything under control.

"When's Nicholas getting here?" I asked.

Rose looked worried. "He should be here by now," she said. "He had some kind of business meeting with his dad. Maybe it ran late."

"The kind of business meeting where they get wild and vampy?" I asked, although those particular meetings usually happened after dark.

"I don't think so," Rose said.

Not only was Nicholas a werewolf, he was a member of the Nightshade City Council. In fact, there was something *different* about all the council members—the town's founding families comprised paranormals of all sorts, including were-wolves, banshees, and vampires. They held their meetings at Mort's Mortuary, the funeral home Nicholas's family owned. Technically, as nonmembers, we weren't even supposed to know about the council and their doings, but Ryan and I had spied on a meeting once.

I heard the door open and Mom's keys jangle.

"We're in here," I called out.

"What's cooking? It smells delicious," Mom said.

"It's almost ready," I said. "Rose, do you think we should wait for Nicholas?"

"No, it's okay," she said.

I was ladling out the soup when the doorbell rang. Rose went to get it. I could tell it was Nicholas by the tone of her voice. I telepathically picked up on a stray thought of hers that made its way into the dining room. *Trouble.* What did Rose mean?

She came back with Nicholas a minute later.

"Hello, Nicholas," Mom said.

"Mrs. Giordano," he said. "Just who I wanted to talk to."

"Mort's Mortuary is having a few problems," Rose explained. "Nicholas and his dad would like us to look into it."

Instead of saying yes, Mom said, "Please sit down. We'll talk about it as we eat."

Poppy helped me to dish up the plates, and then we sat in silence for a moment as we ate.

"What kind of problems?" Mom finally said.

"Things have been . . . out of place," Nicholas admitted.

I asked eagerly, "You think it's something supernatural?" My specialty. "Someone at school mentioned she'd seen lights and heard strange noises coming from the building. What's going on?"

"Let's just say that the Tranquility Room hasn't been very tranquil," he said.

"They're not sure what's causing the disturbance," Rose said. "Mom, can you help them?"

"We can try. I'll see if I can get a reading."

Just then her cell phone went off. "It's Chief Mendez. I'll have to take this." My mom worked with the Nightshade police squad on a lot of cases.

She put the phone to her ear and had a low-voiced conversation. When she hung up, she said, "Nicholas, I'm afraid we'll have to table this for another time. I've been called to a case. But tell your dad the girls and I will be glad to help."

She stood and came over to kiss my forehead. "Daisy, dinner was delicious."

"But you've hardly touched your pasta. And it's your favorite," I protested.

"Save it for me. I'll eat it when I get home." She left the room.

"Let's go over to Mort's and see if we can get a reading," Rose suggested.

"But what about Mom?" Poppy said.

"You heard her," Rose replied. "She said 'the girls and I' will help."

My help? Doubtful. My psychic powers were not the most reliable, even at the best of times.

CHAPTER THREE

When we arrived at Mort's, Nicholas unlocked the door and let us in. I guessed the locked door meant there wasn't a viewing scheduled. Good thing. I'd seen exactly one dead person (or, as it turned out, undead) and I wasn't looking forward to seeing another.

We checked in with Mr. Bone, who was sitting in his office. Not much wiped the smile from Mort's face, but the chaos in the mortuary had left him pale under his golfer's tan. He showed us where the trouble was and retreated quickly. The Tranquility Room was the nicest room at the funeral home, decorated in tasteful beiges. A large fire roared in the fireplace.

"Who lit that fire?" Rose asked.

Nicholas shrugged. "Nobody knows. That's the problem."

"What is that smell?" I asked. It sure wasn't funeral flowers.

"It's cologne," Poppy replied, sniffing the air. "Dreamer by Versace, to be specific."

Since when had she become a men's fragrance expert? Then I remembered the parade of one-time-onlys that had crossed our threshold in the past few months. Not one, single guy had been granted a repeat date.

"Which one of your guys used that?"

She stared at me for a minute. "None of them," she said. "Don't you remember? It's what Dad always smelled like."

I tried not to wince. I didn't remember. In fact, I didn't want to remember.

"I guess that means our ghost is most likely a male," Rose said.

"Do you think it's him?" Poppy said hopefully.

"No, Poppy, I don't think it's our dead father paying us a long-overdue visit," I snapped. "In the first place, he's probably living in Ohio with some woman, a pack of kids, and a minivan."

I could feel someone watching me. The hair on the back of my neck stood up. We weren't alone. A large vase on the mantel started to shake. The vase rocked faster and faster until it flew off the mantel and whizzed by my head. It crashed to the floor and shattered.

I turned to Poppy. "Did you do that?" I thought she might be playing tricks with her telekinesis again. But she wouldn't scare the heck out of me just for kicks. Humiliate me, yes. Like when I borrowed one of her sweaters without permission, and it floated off me during my first date, leaving me hanging in the breeze.

Poppy looked pale and frightened. "No way!"

"This sort of thing has been happening constantly," Nicholas said. "The room is unusable."

"Looks like a textbook haunting to me," Rose said.

The fire roared higher and higher until I thought it was going to jump out of the hearth. Despite the heat of the flames, the room was terribly cold.

Suddenly, the fire went out, leaving the room full of smoke. When it cleared, I saw Poppy picking up a small piece of paper off the floor.

"Look at this," she said to us. "It's a funeral card. For a guy named Gage Atwood. He died last year around this time."

Rose peered at the card. "Amazing," she murmured.

"Whoever he is, he seems pretty ticked off," I said, looking at the shards of broken glass littering the floor.

"Can we check your dad's records for Gage Atwood?" Rose asked Nicholas. "It might help us if we find out how he died."

They left the Tranquility Room, leaving me with a troubled-looking Poppy.

"I'm sorry what I said before—about Dad." I said quietly. The truth was, we didn't know whether he was living or dead. But either way, he was gone.

"It's okay," she said, grabbing a tissue from a box on a small side table. It was a funeral home, after all. The place was littered with them. "I just need to be alone for a few minutes."

"Here?" I looked around the room. I could still feel a presence. "I don't know if you're alone, exactly."

"I don't mind," Poppy said.

"Are you sure it's okay to leave you?"

"He threw a vase at you, not me." She waved me off. "Go ahead. I'll see you at Slim's."

I left her in the wrecked room but stood in the hallway out of sight for a few seconds before leaving. It sounded like Poppy was trying to talk to the ghost. I checked my watch and finally decided she'd be safe enough. Rose, Nicholas, and Mr. Bone were there if she got into any real trouble.

If I'd had any idea what was going to happen, I would never have left her alone with a ghost. Not for a second. So much for my psychic skills.

CHAPTER FOUR

Slim's was your basic fifties-type diner. Red-leather booths, lots of stainless steel, and a permanent greasy smell. One of the servers was Flo, a fixture at Slim's, who waited on you if and when she felt like it. If you ever had the nerve to hand her a pink uniform, she would have handed you your head on a platter, with a little garnish of parsley.

Flo was in her early twenties, with serious tats. Her uniform consisted of blue jeans and a variety of T-shirts. Today's shirt read, come to the dark side. i have cookies.

The diner was crowded, and I spotted a bunch of kids from school clustered around Duke at a booth in the back. I wasn't in the mood to worship the new guy—fortunately, there were still a few empty tables by the door. I sat down to wait for Poppy. The door jingled and I looked up. It was a stranger, a girl about my own age. She had long dark hair and gorgeous full lips, but it was her unusual amber eyes that sent a shiver through me. She hurried to the counter to pick up a to-go order.

"Three rare steaks, right?" I heard her ask Flo.

The jukebox abruptly kicked on, although no one had put in any money. None of the regular clientele even looked up. Everyone at Slim's was getting used to the jukebox's weird ways. It played whatever it wanted, whenever it wanted to play it. The song it had decided on this time was "Lovers and Liars" by Matchbook Romance. Sometimes I felt like the jukebox—which I liked to call Lil—was trying to send me messages with its song choices, but I didn't always quite get what it was trying to tell me. As I pondered the meaning, the mysterious girl slipped past me out of the diner and into the night.

Duke spotted me sitting alone and broke free from his clinging admirers.

"Daizee," he said. He practically had to bodycheck Penny to get her off his arm. He came rushing over.

"Hi, Duke." He was everywhere these days.

"Would you like to join us? I'm reading tea leaves for some of my new friends."

"Uh, thanks, but I'm waiting for my sister."

"I would be honored if you would introduce us," he said. He looked so hopeful that I couldn't say no.

"Sure," I said. "She should be here any minute."

Just then, Poppy walked in and plopped down in a chair. I noticed she had a rather large bandage on her hand.

"What happened?" I asked anxiously. I was ready to kill

that ghost for hurting my sister, except for the obvious fact that he was already dead.

"It's nothing."

"It doesn't look like nothing."

Poppy shot me a warning look and then looked at Duke. "Are you going to introduce me to your friend, Daisy?"

"Oh, yeah, this is Duke Sherrad," I said, still distracted by the thought of a violent ghost.

"So pleased to meet you, Poppy," Duke said, and kissed her unbandaged hand. She blushed. This guy didn't quit. After charming my sister for a few minutes, he said, "Please excuse me. I need to obtain fresh tea leaves for the reading."

"The reading?" Poppy said it with a straight face, but she had a gleam in her eyes when she looked at me.

I glanced at an imaginary spot above her head. It wasn't polite to laugh in someone's face. "Flo will get you a tea bag if you ask."

"I have my own loose tea," he explained, "but I need a fresh cup and some hot water."

He'd passed the first test. If he would have used a tea bag instead of the proper loose tea, it would have given him away as a phony.

As soon as Duke left the table, I went back to hounding Poppy about her injury. "So what did that ghost do to you?" I demanded.

"He was just a little . . . irritated, what with being dead and all, but we came to an understanding."

"Did he happen to mention what's got him in an uproar?"

"Nope, but I read him the riot act. He helped me clean up."

"He what?"

Poppy looked at me with amusement. "Just because he's incorporeal doesn't mean he shouldn't have to take responsibility for being a jerk."

She looked especially pretty with some color in her cheeks. She was wearing a hoodie that exactly matched her eyes. Ghost or plain old guy, he was no match for Poppy's big blue eyes. She glanced over to where Duke was leaning on the counter. "So what's up with this new guy?" she asked. "He's hot. And he seems rather anxious to please you."

"Unlike my boyfriend." I muttered it underneath my breath, but Poppy heard me.

She raised an eyebrow. "Trouble in paradise?"

"It's nothing," I said.

She raised her eyebrows. "It doesn't sound like nothing to me," she said.

I gave in. "It's just that . . . Ryan hasn't asked me to prom yet. And I think something else might be wrong—"

Just then, Duke came back with a steaming teapot and cups. "First the tea must steep," he announced. "You must drink it first. It is the finest tea from China."

"Me?" I said. "No way. I'm not doing it."

Poppy mouthed, "Chicken."

I glared at her and then snatched up the teacup. "I'll do it." I blew on the tea gently to cool it and then sipped it slowly.

"Now take the cup and swish it like this." Duke demonstrated by cupping my hand in his. His hand lingered as he did it, and Poppy stared at us as if mesmerized.

I handed him the cup, and he peered into it.

"I see a chain," he said. "It's broken, I'm afraid."

"So?"

"It means that you have a hidden enemy," Duke said.

I glanced across the restaurant at Penny, who glared daggers at us. Maybe my enemy wasn't exactly hidden, after all. I relaxed my shoulders. Big deal, Penny Edwards didn't like me. It wasn't going to make headlines, not even in the front pages of the *Nightshade Gazette*.

Poppy was chattering away to Duke. It wasn't hard to figure out that Duke was a flirt, but I was a little miffed that he'd transferred his interest from me to my sister so easily. He was a good listener, though. He didn't talk much about himself, but instead spent the whole time asking Poppy about herself.

The bell jingled over the front door again, and I looked up, hoping to see Ryan. But it was only a couple of the teachers from school.

A minute later, Duke said, "Please excuse me. It has been a pleasure to become more well acquainted with the two of you, but I have seen someone I must speak with."

After he left our table, I used the opportunity to try to convince a reluctant Poppy to head for home. I wanted to look something up. Did a broken chain even symbolize a hidden enemy, or was Duke bluffing?

She glanced around Slim's, and I knew she was looking for Duke, but there was no sign of him. He must have slipped out when we weren't looking.

"I made peach ice cream," I coaxed. It was Poppy's favorite, so we were soon headed back to our house.

Rose and Mom still weren't back when we got home. Mom always said she worked late on this or that case, but I wondered if she spent some of her time doing something else. It had even crossed my mind that she was dating Chief Mendez on the sly. They did spend a lot of time together, but somehow I just couldn't quite picture it, especially since I was dating his son.

And a part of me didn't like the idea of someone replacing my father, even though he'd been the one to leave. Or vanish, to be completely accurate. One minute, my father was a devoted, loving husband and dad; the next, he was just . . . gone. The rumors swirled that he'd abandoned us for another woman, but we never found out for sure.

Maybe that's what Mom was up to. Whatever she was doing, I was sure she was hiding something.

I combed our bookshelves looking for a book on tea reading, but I couldn't find anything.

"Poppy, have you seen a book about fortune-telling any-where?" I called out. "I was sure Mom had one here."

"Mom isn't some hack like your friend at the diner," Poppy said, emerging from the kitchen, her mouth full of peach ice cream. "She's a professional." I guessed my sister's infatuation with Duke was over. Poppy could be temperamental, but she was usually a pretty good judge of guys.

I continued scanning the shelves. Mom had tons of books on the paranormal, a couple on police procedures, a few novels, and Dad's old textbooks. I avoided those, then finally found what I was looking for. *The Big Book of Fortune-Telling* told me that a broken chain did indeed mean a hidden enemy. But did that mean Duke was the real deal or just good at research?

The next morning, I saw Ryan in the quad during the mid-morning break.

"Daisy, there's something I want to talk to you about," he said.

Duke Sherrad's arrival interrupted Ryan's train of thought.

"Daizee, how are you this morning? I was unavoidably de-tained last night and couldn't return to continue our talk."

"It's okay, really," I said.

"What conversation?" Ryan said.

"Poppy and I ran into Duke at Slim's last night."

Ryan frowned but didn't say anything. I could tell he was upset.

When the bell rang, Duke walked with me to class. Ryan didn't. He stomped off in the other direction, with a curt "See you after school." I wanted to remind him that he'd see me in gym class, but I didn't think he was in the mood for any smart remarks.

I could count on the fingers of one hand how many months we'd been dating, but he was taking me for granted already?

I sulked my way through statistics and then stomped off to enjoy lunch by myself, but Duke caught up with me.

"Daizee, please allow me to take you to lunch to apologize for abandoning you. I did not mean to leave you or your charming sister." He looked so earnest that I couldn't say no. I didn't have any plans with Ryan or anything. Besides, it was a bit of a pleasure to get Penny's nose out of joint. She was hovering so hard that I finally took pity on her, though.

"Penny, would you like to join us?"

She shrugged but then trailed after us to stand in the lunch line. To my surprise, Ryan was right in front of us. He grabbed my hand. "Hey, sorry I was so grumpy earlier. I'll buy you lunch to make up for it."

Why was everyone suddenly trying to feed me? "I'm having lunch with Duke—and Penny," I added hurriedly when his face started to cloud. "Why don't you join us?"

He grabbed his tray and went to pay without a backward glance. I sighed. I wasn't any good at this relationship stuff. Where was Samantha when I needed her? She had Sean wrapped around her well-manicured finger, and I needed boyfriend tips.

Luckily, Ryan and I had a standing date on Tuesdays after school—it was the only day he didn't have baseball practice. Today we were going to have the house to ourselves. Poppy had gone back to Mort's for some reason, Mom was at a forensics seminar in Santa Cruz, and Rose was out with Nicholas.

I raced around the kitchen. I wanted the night to be perfect. I felt like I hadn't spent any time alone with Ryan in forever. I was sure we'd be able to clear up all our misunderstandings after a little quality time together. Maybe he'd even take this opportunity to finally ask me to the prom.

When the doorbell rang, I smoothed my hands down the front of my apron to wipe away my suddenly sweaty palms, then took off the apron and went to the door.

I opened it, expecting to see Ryan, but no one was there. I peered out into the night. I would have sworn that I had heard the doorbell.

Out of the corner of my eye, I saw something moving in the bushes near the front gate. There was a strange snuffling noise and then a squeal, which was abruptly cut off.

I shivered as I closed the door. It dawned on me that I was alone in the house, vulnerable to whatever was out there. I shook the thought off. I was perfectly safe, I told myself. But I still made sure to bolt the door.

The doorbell rang again a few minutes later, and this time

Ryan stood in my doorway. But he looked stiff and uncomfortable, almost like this was a first date again.

I invited him in, but he just stood there.

"Is something wrong, Ryan?"

He doubled over, grabbing at his stomach as if in a huge amount of pain.

I put my hand to his forehead. He was burning up.

"Uh," he managed to get out, "I'm not feeling well. We'll have to reschedule."

"Ryan, let me drive you to the doctor or something. You have a fever."

"No!" he said. "I'll . . . I'll be fine. It's just a bad . . . case of the stomach flu."

It looked like more than the flu to me. His skin had been hot to the touch, and his complexion looked gray. He was shivering uncontrollably.

Before I could do anything else, he bolted, got into his car, and drove away.

I stared after him in disbelief for several minutes, then went inside and shut the door. Boys. Sometimes they were the biggest mystery of all.

CHAPTER FIVE

Ryan wasn't in school the next day. I walked through the day in a daze. Had he been telling the truth? Was he really sick or just sick of me?

I was incredibly relieved when the long, dull day ended and I could go home and hide. Poppy was in the kitchen when I got there.

"Thanks for the ride," I said as I threw my backpack down.

"Someone's in a bad mood," Poppy observed.

I ignored her and got out a bag of popcorn kernels. I'd make popcorn the old-fashioned way—on the stove. But I couldn't concentrate. Instead of cooking, I paced the length of the kitchen.

I could feel Poppy staring at me. "What's wrong with you?" she finally asked.

"Nothing." I slammed the corn popper on the burner.

Poppy snorted in disbelief. "You've been moping around all day!"

"I have not!" I said. The bag of kernels exploded into a blizzard of white, fluffy popcorn and rained down on the kitchen.

"Nothing, huh?" Poppy said. She caught a piece of the flying popcorn in her mouth.

My psychic powers went wonky when I was under stress. Part of me was mad at myself—getting all revved up over some guy. But Ryan wasn't just any guy. We'd been friends way before we dated, before I'd been a cheerleader, before Sam and I became friends again. There were times when Ryan had been the only person I had to confide in.

"Okay," I said. "I'm a little . . . preoccupied. It's just that Ryan's been acting really weird lately."

I told her about our failed date and how sick Ryan had seemed. "And he wasn't in school today and hasn't been answering his cell. And he *still* hasn't asked me to the prom yet."

"Geez, Daisy," Poppy said. "It's only a few weeks away."

"I'm aware of that," I said.

"Has he asked someone else?" Poppy said. She wasn't exactly known for her tact. Despite all the problems Ryan and I had been having, I hadn't even thought of that.

"I don't know," I said. The idea of Ryan going out with someone else made me feel a little queasy. "Poppy, you're not helping."

"Hey, I've got an idea," she said. "Let's grab the Frisbee and head to the park. Spending some time outside will make you feel better. And besides, you really ought to work on getting a handle on your telekinesis. Things get out of control when you're upset."

I nodded and grabbed the car keys. What else was there to do?

On our drive to the park, Poppy looked out the window. "There's Ryan," she said, waving madly. "Who is that he's talking to?"

Ryan was standing outside Slim's. Next to him was a tall, beautiful brunette. I slowed down the car as we approached.

It was the girl I'd seen at the diner, the one with the amber eyes. I had no idea who she was, but the two of them were chatting like old friends.

"Are you going to stop?" Poppy asked.

"No," I said, gritting my teeth. The sight of Ryan with another girl made me feel like there was a cement mixer in my stomach.

I'd seen Ryan with another girl before and had completely misinterpreted the situation. Even so, seeing him with someone else again wasn't exactly doing much for my confidence. And besides, wasn't he supposed to be home sick today?

I stomped on the gas and headed for the park. I looked in the rearview mirror and saw the bulbs in the Slim's Diner sign above their heads explode in a cascade of sparks that just missed Ryan and the girl. I hoped I hadn't caused it, but I had the guilty feeling that I might be responsible.

There was silence in the car until we pulled into a parking spot at the park. Then Poppy said, "I'm sure it's nothing."

Right. If it were nothing, she wouldn't be talking about it.

We walked to a secluded area of the park.

"Okay, toss me the Frisbee."

I did. Poppy didn't appreciate it.

"Without using your hands, Daisy. We're here to practice controlling your telekinesis, not to improve your Frisbee skills."

I tried moving it with my mind. My first few attempts resulted in the Frisbee careening off toward the fountain several yards behind Poppy, but I finally got the hang of it.

"Good!" Poppy said as the Frisbee took a perfectly straight path to her hands. "You're getting better."

It was getting dark. Normally, not much in Nightshade spooked me, but I suddenly felt the hairs on the back of my neck stand up. Someone was watching us.

I moved closer to Poppy, until I was right next to her. "Why don't we call it a night? Mom will be waiting for us," I said in what I hoped was a carrying voice.

"Don't quit now," she said. "You're just getting started. Besides, Mom—*ooph*. Hey, watch it." I'd elbowed her in the ribs.

"Someone is watching us," I explained in a low voice. "And I don't want to advertise that no one is expecting us."

Poppy nodded and picked up the Frisbee. "Yeah, we don't want to worry Mom. You know how she gets if we're late." I hoped I hadn't sounded as artificial as she did.

We made a beeline for the car. My skin didn't stop crawling until we pulled into our driveway.

Mom was already home, which was unusual and brought me ever so slightly out of my funk. I couldn't go to my room, not if I wanted to take advantage of the opportunity for some quality time with my one remaining parent.

"It smells great in here, Mom," I said as Poppy and I entered the kitchen.

"I felt like cooking tonight," she replied. "It's just salad and baked chicken."

"Sounds good to me." It was nice to have a night off from cooking.

Mom glanced over at Poppy and frowned. "What happened to your hand?"

Poppy and I exchanged glances. I raised an eyebrow and shrugged. It was up to her.

"It was the ghost at Mort's," she finally said. "He was busting stuff up, and I got in the way."

"This ghost sounds dangerous," Mom said sharply. "I don't know if you girls should be handling this."

"It's nothing," Poppy said. "And besides, he calmed down after I talked to him."

"Let me see your hand," Mom said.

"It's just a scratch," Poppy said, but she obediently held out her hand. "I told you."

After a thorough inspection, Mom said, "It looks okay, but

remember to put some ointment on it." She turned to me and said, "Ghosts can be unpredictable. Are you sure you girls have this under control?"

Seeing Poppy's pleading look, I nodded, though I wasn't so sure about it myself. "Everything is fine, Mom, don't worry," I said.

Just as we were about to sit down to eat, Rose came in and eased everyone's worries. "Mr. Bone sent this as a thanks." She handed Poppy and me small packages. "He hasn't had any more ghost trouble."

"Really?" Mom said, sounding impressed.

"You make him sound like a pest," Poppy protested.

"He was one," Rose said. "A big one, but Poppy managed to tame him."

Poppy ripped open her package and held up a big box of Donnelly chocolates. Donnelly's was in Santa Cruz and made the best chocolates. I resisted the urge to snatch the box out of her hands and snarf the contents. Chocolate is my weakness.

"Oh, I think he likes you," I teased.

"He does?" Poppy beamed. Not exactly the reaction we were expecting. Mr. Bone isn't exactly pinup material. "I'll have to thank Gage."

"Gage?" I asked incredulously. "I meant Mr. Bone."

I stared at Poppy, who was turning even pinker.

"You thought we were talking about the ghost!" Rose exclaimed.

"No, it's just—he's nice, that's all. He was only seventeen when he died. He listened to me."

"Poppy, he's a ghost. He's a captive audience," I emphasized. I wasn't trying to be mean, but I was worried.

"I'm tired of the guys at school," she said.

"Talk about a long-distance relationship. It'll never work," I said.

Rose giggled and then sobered quickly when Poppy turned to her and glared.

"Like either of you is doing any better," she said. "You and Ryan aren't even talking, and Rose's boyfriend is a . . ."

I gave Rose a panic-stricken look. Mom didn't know Nicholas was a werewolf.

"A what, Poppy?" Rose's voice was calm, but her face was a little pale.

"C'mon, you guys," I said, attempting to change the subject, "we shouldn't be fighting."

Mom was on full alert now. "Finish your sentence, Poppy."

"A mortician," Poppy finally said.

"I thought you were going to say something else," Mom said, raising an eyebrow. "You know Poppy, a person can't help it if he has Were blood. There's no reason to belittle him."

Due to her line of work, Mom was pretty tight with the

city council members. She took offense to any sort of paranormal discrimination.

"Sorry," Poppy mumbled, looking at Rose apologetically. "I didn't mean to insult your boyfriend."

Rose relaxed a fraction, but Mom was chewing on something else Poppy had blurted out.

"Why aren't you and Ryan talking, Daisy?"

"It's nothing, Mom. Really." But was it nothing? Poppy had been reassuring in the car, but a few seconds ago, when she was mad, she seemed to be implying that my relationship was reaching the crash-and-burn stage. I wondered if she was right.

"Are you sure you don't want to talk about it?" Mom asked, seeing the troubled look on my face.

I gave in to the female bonding instinct and blurted out my worries. "It's just that he bailed out of our date last night because he was sick, but then Poppy and I spotted him outside Slim's this afternoon."

"Did he have a fever?" Rose asked.

I said yes. How did she know?

"How high was his temperature?"

"I don't know," I replied. "He left before I could take it. But I felt his forehead, and it felt like he was on fire. Why?"

"No reason," she said. "I just heard there's a really nasty strain of flu going around. He'll be fine, just give him a few days."

"A few days?" I scoffed. "He looked perfectly healthy when I saw him today."

"Daisy, I'm sure there's an explanation. Just be patient," Rose said.

My sister said it with such authority that I persuaded myself she was right. I managed a smile.

"Okay, who wants popcorn?" I asked. "Maybe I'll add M&Ms."

We spent the evening hanging out in the family room. Ryan didn't call, and I didn't call him.

When the phone finally rang, I looked anxiously at the number on the caller ID. Samantha. I knew from past experience that if I didn't answer, she'd just keep calling or maybe even come over.

I picked up the phone. "What's up, Samantha?"

"I looked for you in the afternoon but couldn't find you anywhere," she said. "You aren't mad at me, are you?"

"I'm not mad." I wasn't, not at Samantha anyway. And there were a thousand good reasons that Ryan could have been with that girl. I just couldn't think of any right now. And a couple of not-so-good ones, my traitorous brain added.

"Hey, did you hear?" she asked.

"Hear what?"

"Another one of Duke's predictions came true. He predicted that Pamela Ellington would be valedictorian, and guess what they announced at the student council meeting today?"

"That Pam Ellington is class valedictorian? I could have told you that."

"And he predicted that Candy and Damon would break up."

"Another easy one to guess," I said.

"Daisy, I thought you of all people would believe in Duke."

"I believe that the psychic phenomenon exists. I'm reserving judgment about his abilities."

Samantha changed the subject, evidently tired of arguing with me about Duke. "So we're on for hanging prom posters tomorrow afternoon?"

After agreeing, I hung up the phone and turned to Poppy.

"What are you doing after school tomorrow?" I asked.

"Forget it," she said. "I already have plans. Besides, I had to do all the work last year. This year, I'm a senior and you get to wait on me."

It was school tradition that the juniors planned the prom and provided all the labor. The seniors just showed up and looked glamorous, at least according to Poppy.

"Who is in charge of the after party?" she asked.

"What after party?"

"The one the juniors had better be planning unless they want to die a slow, agonizing death."

Alrighty then. Looked like, on top of everything else, we had a party to plan.

CHAPTER SIX

The next day after school, the prom committee followed Samantha to the art room, where the posters were stored. We gathered up the posters and supplies while Sam barked orders.

"We should split up into groups of two," Samantha said.

Penny stepped forward with an eager smile, but Samantha continued like she hadn't even seen her. "Daisy, you're with me. Penny, you're with Rachel." Sam divided up the rest of the girls and ended with a final order. "I want to see posters everywhere you look. We still have a load of prom tickets to sell, and I've heard that some people don't even have dates yet."

I was going to kill her if she looked my way, but fortunately for her safety, she didn't. "Let's go, people!"

As we walked down the hall, we were stopped every few feet by someone who wanted to talk to Samantha.

First, Mrs. Pappas, the yearbook committee adviser, rushed after us. "Samantha, do you have a minute to look at the layout?" she asked.

"I'll come by tomorrow, I promise," Samantha assured her.

Finally, after being stopped by the prom committee adviser, the debate team adviser, and Principal Amador, who just wanted to say hi, we started hanging posters.

"When do you sleep?" I said.

"What do you mean?" Samantha replied. She stuck a poster on the wall and stepped back to take a look.

"You're involved in everything," I said. "When do you have time to just hang out at home?"

Her face fell, and I realized I'd put my foot in my mouth again. Samantha's parents were never home. She was alone in that big house most of the time.

"Sam, I didn't mean . . ."

She gave me a strained smile. "I like to keep busy," she said. "Don't you? Isn't that why you joined prom committee?"

"I guess," I said. "Poppy said something last night about planning an after party for the seniors. I guess it's the juniors' job?"

Samantha nodded. "One more thing to do." She sighed as she looked thoughtfully at the poster on the wall in front of us. "You know, Daisy," she said, "You're right. I do have a lot on my plate right now. Do you want to take charge of planning the after-prom party?"

"I've never done anything like that before," I told her, "and Poppy will kill me if it's not perfect. It's her senior prom. Last chance to make memories and all that."

"You'll do a great job," she said. "And I'll help you. I'll get the whole committee to help."

I thought about it for a minute. I needed a project to take my mind off Ryan anyway. "Okay, I'll do it."

Samantha and I ended up by the boys' locker rooms. "We should put a bunch here," she said. "Some boys need a little prompting." She glanced at me, a question in her gaze.

"Ryan hasn't asked me yet. I don't know what's up with him. Do you?"

"No," Samantha said, but she wouldn't look at me when she said it. She knew something, I was sure of it. Her boyfriend Sean was Ryan's best friend.

"He's been acting weird lately," I said, watching her closely. Then, after looking around to make sure Penny wasn't lurking behind some corner, I admitted: "Sam, I saw him with another girl."

Her eyes widened. "What do you mean? Who was it?"

"I don't know her," I said, "But I saw her at Slim's the other night. Long dark hair, lips like Angelina Jolie, and these weird yellowish eyes."

"That sounds like Elise Wilder," Sam said. "Total femme fatale."

"You know her?" I asked incredulously.

"I met her back when I went up to the Wilder mansion to book it for prom."

"Elise Wilder," I said. "Why haven't I ever met her before

now? I know everybody in Nightshade." I've lived here my whole life and I'd never heard anyone mention her name.

"She's been going to finishing school in Europe," Samantha said.

"What brings her to Nightshade?" I asked.

"She's kind of wild," Samantha said. "Her grandmother, Mrs. Wilder, has sent her to about a dozen schools, and she's managed to get kicked out of every one. She'll be finishing her senior year at Nightshade High."

Great. Just great.

The very next day, I came face-to-face with my rival.

Samantha and I were manning the cupcake decorating station to raise money for the prom and the after party. I had baked and frosted the cupcakes, and everyone could decorate their own. Sam and I set up a table during lunch on Friday afternoon and waited for hungry students to dig in.

"So have you given any thought to the after party?" Sam asked.

I nodded enthusiastically. I had done some serious brainstorming the night before. "I was thinking of something like a Dark Carnival theme." It was amazing the things one could come up with when sitting at home, dateless.

"Dark Carnival?"

"You know, moody lighting, kind of creepy."

"Will there be clowns? Because I've always thought clowns were totally creepy."

"We could have different booths," I suggested. "With carnival games and stuff."

"We can get Duke to read fortunes," she said. "If he's not too busy." She sent me a sly glance.

"Cut it out, Sam," I said. "I'm *not* going to the prom with Duke."

"So where are we going to have this soiree?" Samantha asked.

"Somewhere outside," I said. "I was thinking your yard might be a good spot. You guys have, like, two acres or something, right?"

Samantha bristled. "No way," she said sharply. "Not my yard."

I was surprised she was down on the idea. After all, the Devereaux house was no stranger to parties. But I knew Sam had been having some family problems recently, so I didn't push the issue.

"What about the park?" Samantha suggested. "There's plenty of room there."

"Maybe," I said, "but wouldn't we have to get, like, permits and stuff?"

"Probably," said Samantha. "But how hard can that be? Your boyfriend's dad is chief of police."

My heart sunk when she mentioned Ryan. Wasn't this prom-planning stuff supposed to keep my mind off him? I reached for an M&M and popped it into my mouth.

"And I thought *I* had strong cravings," someone observed. I looked up and saw Elise Wilder.

Her dark hair was pulled back into a ponytail, revealing a triangular face and drawing attention to her thickly arched brows and strange eyes. She looked sleek and dangerous, like a hungry cat looking at a mouse. She wore an expensive pair of trendy jeans so hard to get that a certain cheerleader I knew would give her left pom-pom to own a pair.

I cleared my throat, realizing I was staring. I was surprised to see her. Two new students enrolling at Nightshade High in one week must be some kind of record. When Duke Sherrad arrived, his picture was on the front page of the school newspaper. Of course, that could be because the student editor, Tim Sullivan, had a well-known fondness for dark-haired hotties. Didn't we all?

"Hi, Elise," Samantha said sweetly. "Have you met Daisy?"

She narrowed her eyes and shook her head.

"You're Ryan's friend, right?" I said it with a confidence I didn't feel. I wondered if "friend" was the right word if her cravings included something along the lines of a tall dark guy with green eyes.

"Friend? Yes, I guess you could call me a friend."

"I'm Daisy Giordano, his . . ." I wasn't sure what I was, not anymore. Not with this absolutely stunning girl standing in front of me.

Elise's eyes focused on the silver acorn ring I was wearing. Grandma Giordano had given it to me.

"Nice ring," she said. She stepped away from me. "You're selling prom tickets here, right?" she asked Samantha.

"Yes," Sam said cheerfully.

Elise nonchalantly whipped a $100 bill out of her wallet and handed it to Sam. "I'll take two."

I couldn't believe she already had a prom date. I wondered who it could be.

"Bye, Elise! Thanks a lot," said Samantha as Elise left the table.

"You're pretty friendly with her," I observed.

A guilty look crossed Sam's face. "I'm trying to convince her to join the cheerleading squad, but she's not interested."

I felt a stab of jealousy. "I didn't realize she had started school here yet," I said glumly.

"Just this morning," Sam said. "She had a town car drop her off. Pretty classy, right?"

I shrugged. *Classy* isn't the word that came to mind when I thought of Elise Wilder.

As if on cue, Poppy approached our table. "Did you see her? The new girl?"

"That's her," I said. "The one we saw Ryan with in front of Slim's."

"I thought so," she replied. "She's gorgeous."

Like I needed to hear that. Leave it to Poppy. She realized what she'd said and added, "Not as pretty as you, of course."

I gave her a little punch on the arm. "Thanks."

"Hey, I need to ask you a favor."

"Shoot."

"Can you call Cassandra or Chelsea and get ahold of a San Carlos yearbook? Last year preferably." Cassandra and Chelsea were twins who went to San Carlos High. We'd met them a few months ago during a case.

"I'll call them tonight," I promised. "But what do you want a San Carlos yearbook for?"

"Gage went there," she said shyly. "And I want to see what he looked like . . . before."

"Oh." Why was Poppy torturing herself? On the other hand, what would it be like to have only a shadowy idea of what your crush looked like?

After kids finished their lunches, they bought and decorated cupcakes. The bake sale was a hit, but I was still worrying about who Elise's prom date could be. My worries were eased when Ryan approached the table, smiling widely.

"What are you up to tonight?" he asked me as he handed me cash for a cupcake.

I shrugged, not wanting to seem too eager. "I don't have any plans yet," I said.

"Why don't I come by your house after baseball practice?"

he asked. "It's been a while since we've spent any real time together."

My heart fluttered when I thought of spending time alone with Ryan. "Sounds good. I'll stop by Slim's and get us a couple of sandwiches for dinner."

Before leaving, he leaned in for a kiss.

"Sweet," Samantha said when he was gone. "But he still hasn't purchased any prom tickets."

Nevertheless, I went through the day smiling.

CHAPTER SEVEN

After school, I ran to Slim's for a couple of deli sandwiches and an order of fries.

As Poppy requested, I made the call to Chelsea, who said
she'd drop the yearbook by the house over the weekend.

"I'll just leave it on the porch if you're not there," she said
gaily.

"Thanks, Chelsea, I owe you."

"Not half as much as I owe you, but I'm curious—what
do you want a San Carlos yearbook for?" she said.

I explained about Gage and Poppy. I knew Chelsea would
understand.

"I remember Gage Atwood," she said. "It was awful what
happened to him."

"What *did* happen to him?"

"Car accident, two weeks before his senior prom," she said.
"He was alone in the car. Hit a tree."

"That's awful," I said.

"Tell me about it."

After I hung up with Chelsea, I started on my homework to kill some time.

But by seven thirty, there was still no sign of Ryan. Baseball was long over. I confirmed it by peeking out the window. Yes, there was Sean's car. He was home, but where was Ryan?

I'd been stood up. There'd better be blood involved. It wasn't like Ryan not to call if he'd gotten tied up.

I decided to be rational and call his cell. Maybe there had been an emergency, or maybe he'd been hurt or something. No answer. I slammed my phone closed and then bolted out the front door, resisting the impulse to slam it, too.

Sam and Sean were hanging on his front porch. I decided to go over and fish for possible information about Ryan's whereabouts.

"Hey," Samantha said. "Ryan leave already?"

"He never showed," I admitted.

She glanced over at Sean. "You know anything about that?"

He wouldn't meet her eyes. "He was still at practice when I left."

There goes the possible dazed-and-bleeding theory.

"You can't let him take you for granted like that. You had *plans* and he just stood you up." She put her hand on her hip and glared at Sean like he had stood *her* up.

I nodded. "Maybe there's a reasonable explanation?" I said weakly. It was hard to argue with Samantha, especially when, in theory, I agreed with her.

Her eyes narrowed. "Don't make excuses for him," she said.

I was tired of thinking about it. I headed to bed, telling myself that things would be better in the morning.

They weren't. Poppy knocked on my bedroom door at the crack of dawn. "Daisy, wake up," she hissed.

I leaned over and blearily checked the time. "Poppy, it's not even five yet. Go back to bed." I rolled over and pulled the covers over my head.

The next thing I knew, Poppy was bouncing up and down on my bed. "Get. Up."

I sat up and threw a pillow at her, which she ducked with the expertise that comes with years of practice. Then I tried to go back to sleep.

"Rose didn't come home last night," Poppy said.

"What do you mean, Rose didn't come home last night?" I repeated, still groggy.

Poppy looked terrible, like she had been up all night. "Daisy, wake up!" she insisted. "I need you coherent."

"Has she done it before?" I asked.

"Well, duh," Poppy said, looking at me like I was stupid. "But she's never stayed out all night before."

I wasn't stupid, just not in the loop. This was just another thing my sisters had kept from me. Poppy and Rose had always been close. For the longest time, I had been an outsider in my own family, the only one without any powers. A norm, like my father.

I still didn't understand what Poppy was so worked up about. "Rose is in college," I said. "What's the big deal?"

"The big deal is tonight is a full moon," Poppy said urgently.

I was wide awake as soon as the realization set in. "Have you tried her cell?"

"About a dozen times," Poppy snapped. "And I called Nicholas, too. They're not answering."

"Did she mention where they were going last night?"

"No, but I know she was heading out to meet him."

"What was Rose doing with Nicholas on the night of a full moon?"

"Shh, keep your voice down," Poppy cautioned me. "You'll wake Mom."

"What are we going to do?" I said.

"We're going to go look for them," she replied. "You get dressed. I'll get the car keys."

"And leave a note for Mom," I told her. "Tell her we're going to Slim's. The least you can do is buy me a cup of coffee."

And maybe I could get a hint or two from my favorite cryptic jukebox.

After I became halfway coherent (or as coherent as I got at five in the morning), we got in the car.

"Where should we look first?" Poppy asked as she backed out of the driveway.

"After we stop for coffee, we'll check Mort's. It's the most logical place to start."

Poppy pulled the car into a parking space right in front of Slim's. The sign was still broken and hanging slightly askew.

"I'll wait in the car," Poppy said.

"Fine, do you want anything?"

"Extra-large Coke, please, lots of ice."

And she thought *I* was addicted to caffeine?

It was early, but there were already a couple of coffee drinkers at the counter.

Flo was on duty. She looked slightly hungover, but then again, it could just have been Flo being Flo. Today her shirt read, LIVE AND UNCENSORED.

"What can I get you?"

I gave her our order.

"You're up awfully early," she commented.

I shrugged. "Early bird gets the werewolf," I said.

"What?"

"Never mind." While Flo made the drinks, I went over to the jukebox, dropped in a quarter, and selected a Springsteen song. I felt a little silly, but I leaned closer and whispered into the jukebox's shiny surface, "Where's my sister?"

To my disappointment, my actual selection came on. Obviously, I wasn't going to get any help there. One of the guys at the counter grumbled something under his breath about my music choice. Who doesn't like the Boss?

I went back to the counter and paid for my drinks. I went

to leave but hesitated when the jukebox cut out and started a new song a second later.

I braced myself for some horrid doom-and-gloom warning, but instead "Good Times" by INXS came on. Was Lil trying to tell me that everything was going to be okay?

As if the jukebox heard my thoughts, "Good Time" cut off and "Walking with a Ghost" by Tegan and Sara came on. Definitely a message for Poppy this time.

Flo stared at me. "You want something else?"

"No," I said. "You haven't happened to see Rose in here, have you? Or Nicholas Bone?"

"Her boyfriend, right?"

I nodded.

Flo thought for a minute. "Her boyfriend, maybe around six last night. Right before my shift ended."

"Thanks," I said. As I walked out the door, the strains of "Monsters of Man" by the Living Things came on the jukebox.

I got into the car and handed Poppy her soda. She slurped as we drove the short distance to Mort's.

"Park in the back, "I said. "That's where Nicholas usually parks."

"I *know*," Poppy snapped as she pulled into a spot near the back door. Nicholas's gray Mercedes was parked in the next space.

"They're here!" Poppy said.

We went to the door, but it was locked.

"What are we going to do now?" Rose could be inside, hurt—or worse.

Poppy dug in her purse. "Wait a minute," she said. A minute later, she triumphantly held up a key. "Gage gave it to me so I could come visit anytime I want."

I hesitated. "Maybe we should call Chief Mendez."

"He'll tell Mom," she objected. "Besides, we're already here. It'll take him at least ten minutes to get here. And Gage will help us if we get into a jam." Poppy put the key in the lock and opened the door. The back entrance took us down a hallway. It was dark and quiet, and I didn't dare to breathe.

What always struck me about the funeral home was the deep, unending silence. Nothing moved, but I always felt like someone, or something, was waiting for me.

Poppy found a light switch and flipped it on. Everything looked normal until I saw the pool of blood in the hallway. That's when Poppy started screaming.

CHAPTER EIGHT

At the sound of Poppy's scream, Gage came tearing out of the Tranquility Room as a dark cloud. He saw Poppy and materialized into the shadow of a very handsome young man. He ignored me and focused on Poppy. Gage put his ghostly arms around her, or at least he tried to, but they went right through her.

"Shh! It's okay," he said. He stroked her hair. There was something tender about the way he tried and failed to touch her.

Finally, Poppy's sobs trailed off into little whimpers. I tried not to look at the blood, but its sharp metallic smell hung in the air.

"Did you see what happened here?" I asked Gage.

"The Were was here," he said. "With the girl who looks like you."

"Rose?" I tried to keep the panic out of my voice.

"Someone was waiting. Another Were. There was a struggle. It hurt. So much blood." Gage's voice sounded far-off, and I wondered if he was reliving his own death. He didn't seem to be focused on the here and now, but instead was clearly in a dark place. He screamed and faded in and out for a minute.

"Gage, what's wrong?" Poppy's voice seemed to snap him out of it. He shuddered and resumed his normal ghostly shape.

"It's nothing," he said. "Just a bad memory."

"What should we do?" Poppy said. "Call the hospital?"

"They wouldn't take Nicholas to the hospital," I said. "How would they explain his furry state?"

"Rose wouldn't just let him bleed to death," Poppy replied. "Where would she take him?"

None of us seemed to have the answer, but a moment later, the door opened and Rose entered the hallway. Her face was white and drawn and there was a smudge of what looked like blood across her cheek. She carried a bucket, rags, and cleaning supplies.

I was relieved to see her, but I couldn't help but wonder how hard it was to get Were blood out of carpeting.

We rushed up to her. "Are you all right?"

Poppy grabbed her and held her tight.

"I'm fine," she said. Then gently, "Poppy, honey, if you don't stop squeezing me, I won't be able to breathe."

Poppy loosened her grasp and stepped back to stare at Rose. "What happened?" She demanded.

Rose dropped to her knees and dabbed at the blood. She avoided looking at any of us, especially me. "I want to get this stain out before it sets."

"Is Nicholas okay? Where is he?" Poppy flooded her with questions, but I didn't say anything. I watched Rose closely, though. Something was wrong. She was hiding something.

"He's fine," she said. "Just a couple of stitches. I took him to a doctor in town, a Were. She stitched him up, and Nicholas is home in bed, resting."

"How did he get hurt?"

"It was nothing. Just an accident." That didn't sound like my sister, brushing off her boyfriend's injury. There was definitely something she wasn't telling us.

For the first time, I deliberately tried to read Rose's mind. I got a quick glimpse of Nicholas being attacked by a younger, lanky Were before Rose slammed down her defenses and kicked me out.

She glared at me and sent me a message. *Do that again and you will regret it.* I could tell she meant it.

Sorry, I sent back. I wouldn't do it again, of course, but I was fascinated by what I'd learned.

There was a teenaged Were in Nightshade? I had seen a few Weres when Ryan and I were spying on the Nightshade City Council one time, but they had all been older looking. Who was the other Were? And why had he and Nicholas been fighting?

These were the questions running through my mind as I spent the rest of the morning helping my sisters scrub the blood out of the carpet at Mort's.

CHAPTER NINE

My cell phone rang several times over the weekend. It was always Ryan's number flashing on the screen, but I ignored it. He probably had a good explanation for skipping our date, but I wasn't in the mood to hear it.

By Monday morning I still hadn't returned his calls. There was no sign of him, but the halls were fairly humming with innuendo and speculation. In the heart of it all stood Penny Edwards, surrounded by a twittering crowd of girls. I went over to join them.

"Did you hear, Daisy? Another one of Duke's predictions came true," she said, teary eyed. "Mr. Davis is dead."

"What happened? When?" Although he wasn't my favorite teacher at Nightshade, I was freaked out by the news.

"Over the weekend. No one knows the details yet," Sam replied.

"But we heard he might have been murdered," Jordan Kelley said. "They found his body by the fountain in the park."

An image of all that blood soaking into the carpet at Mort's flashed in my mind. Was Rose telling me the truth about what had happened there?

"But it's just like Duke predicted," Penny insisted. "What do you have to say about that?"

"Duke predicted that something would happen to Mr. Davis?"

"Well, not exactly." Penny tossed her head. "He predicted that there was danger in the trees."

I frowned. The trees? Everyone knew that Mr. Davis went for a run in the park every night. There were lots of trees there.

"I heard he was out jogging," Samantha said. "The guy was more worried about getting middle-aged spread than anybody I knew." There was a disgusted look on her face, but I wasn't sure if it was because of the gossip or because Penny was getting all the attention.

"I heard he had a heart attack and no one found him until morning," Rachel said.

The gossip was flying. Who knew *what* the truth was.

Penny continued to chirp like an annoying little sparrow. "And just think, Duke predicted the whole thing."

I could feel the expression on my face turning skeptical. You'd think I, of all people, would believe in Duke's abilities, wouldn't you? But I'd seen enough fake psychics in my life to have my doubts. After my dad disappeared, the vultures descended on my mom. In her quest to find out what had happened to him, my mom seemed to forget everything she'd learned about the difference between a true psychic and a scam artist. Even worse, her own gift had suffered. She eventually regained most of her sanity and her ability, but not before she'd been taken advantage of, both emotionally and financially.

Just then, Principal Amador's voice broke in over the loudspeaker. "All students, please report to the auditorium for a special assembly."

"What's going on?" I asked Rachel as we gathered up our backpacks and merged into the stream of students headed for the auditorium.

"I dunno," she said. "But I heard there were police everywhere this morning."

"Including Ryan's dad," Penny piped in from behind us. "Didn't he mention it?"

I quickened my pace. Trust Penny to get in a cheap shot. I'm sure she already knew Ryan and I weren't exactly communicating these days.

In the auditorium, several teachers and students were crying. Mr. Davis had been popular. Still no sign of Ryan. But his dad, Chief Mendez, was sitting in a folding chair on stage, next to the podium where Principal Amador stood.

"Good morning," the principal said. "As you have all heard, Dexter Davis was found dead in Nightshade City Park early Saturday morning. The cause of death is unknown, but an autopsy is being performed. He was a great teacher and an important part of the Nightshade community, and he will be greatly missed. This is an upsetting time for all of us. If you wish to speak to a counselor, they will be available all week in Nurse Phillips's office. Now Chief Mendez would like to have a few words with you."

The chief stood at the podium and cleared his throat. "If any of you have any information that will help us catch Mr. Davis's killer, please speak to me or one of my officers after the assembly."

After a short silence, someone called out to Chief Mendez from the audience. It was Christy Hannigan. "Chief Mendez, I heard Mr. Davis was attacked by a wild animal. Is that true?"

The chief looked slightly flustered. "Where did you hear that?"

"My mother was one of the first paramedics on the scene," Christy continued. "She said there were claw marks all over Mr. Davis's face!"

Panic swept through the audience. I digested the news. Christy wasn't usually given to exaggeration.

"Now, let's just keep calm," Chief Mendez said coolly. "It's true that the circumstances of this death are suspicious. Rest assured that the authorities are looking into it and that everything is under control. The residents of Nightshade have nothing to fear."

Nothing to fear but a murderer on the loose. I wondered if Chief Mendez was just acting nonchalant to keep people from panicking or if he was covering up something. I knew that the chief sometimes consulted the Nightshade City Council on crimes where something supernatural was involved. After all, the council made all the decisions for Nightshade's paranormal community. Could the chief be protecting a werewolf?

After the assembly I decided to talk to him. He was conversing quietly with Bane Paxton, who looked shell-shocked. I thought I overheard them say something about "the scourge." They looked up, alarmed, when I approached. Bane quickly excused himself.

"Hanging in there, Daisy?" Chief Mendez asked.

I nodded. "Chief, is Ryan coming to school today?"

"He's out sick today," he said. "I thought he had told you."

Sick *again*?

"Nope." I sighed. Ryan hadn't been telling me much lately, but I wouldn't burden his dad with that grievance. "Thanks for letting me know."

"Daisy," the chief said as I turned to walk away, "don't give up on Ryan. He's just going through some hard times right now. He'll get over it."

Hearing that from Chief Mendez made me feel a little better—but only a little. Who knew what Ryan was hiding from his dad. They hadn't been on the best of terms lately. I smiled weakly.

"Do you really think you'll catch Mr. Davis's killer?" I couldn't resist asking.

The chief became all business. "I'm sure of it, Daisy. Don't you worry about anything. With the police department and your mom on the case, we'll solve this in no time."

"My mom is on the case?" I asked. She hadn't mentioned anything about it to me all weekend.

"I called her first thing this morning," Chief Mendez said. "We're meeting up in a bit so I can fill her in on the details."

My heart sunk, knowing that this meant my mom probably wouldn't be getting home from work early again anytime soon. I shrugged and said, "I guess you can use all the help you can get with this one, huh?"

The chief gave me a suspicious look.

I caught a random thought from him: *Don't get involved.* Solving mysteries ran in my blood. I was anxious to take on this case, but apparently, he didn't think it was a good idea.

All day long, Mr. Davis's death was the subject of every conversation.

Poppy and Rose were in the living room watching a movie when I got home. I could tell by their faces that they'd already heard the news.

"Can you believe it?"

Poppy lowered her voice. "You want to know something? I was hanging out with Gage at Mort's after school today and I heard Nicholas's dad talking about it. They think Mr. Davis's death is City Council business."

I gulped. That confirmed my theory.

"I got the impression they think something *furry* is involved."

"Did Nicholas mention anything to you about Mr. Davis?" I asked Rose.

"No, why would he?" Rose replied, but her voice was high and strained. She was an unconvincing liar.

Did Rose know something? And if so, why was she keeping it from us? I tried to probe her thoughts, but she was shut down. She gave me a cut-it-out look, and I withdrew guiltily. I'd always hated it when Rose wandered into my mind unintentionally. There was no excuse for my deliberate invasion of her privacy.

Sorry, I mouthed. I decided we needed to be up front with Rose. "I heard it was a werewolf attack."

"What?" she gasped. "There's no way it was Nicholas."

"We know that," I reassured her. "We didn't think for a minute that it was. But what about the other werewolves in town?"

"Like who?" Rose asked, eyeing me suspiciously.

It's true that I didn't know exactly who the other Weres in Nightshade were. But I could take a wild guess. "Well . . . how about Mr. Bone? Do you know where he was the night it happened?"

"Mr. Bone?" she said. Then she seemed to get the drift of my thoughts. "Daisy, didn't you know? Nicholas is adopted."

"So?" Poppy said.

"So," I said, slowly understanding what Rose was trying to say. "Mr. Bone isn't a werewolf. But the City Council always meets at Mort's Mortuary. I just assumed that Mr. Bone was on the council."

"He is," Rose admitted. "Think about it. Mr. *Bone.*"

"Mr. Bone is Skull," I said. We'd run into a walking, talking skeleton, whom I nicknamed Skull, when Ryan and I had snuck into a Council meeting. "The leader of the Nightshade City Council," I added for Poppy's benefit. Even I had a hard time believing it. Mr. Bone was a round little man, perpetually sunburnt from spending all his free time playing golf. He did not look like the leader of a paranormal secret society.

"There was a full moon the night Mr. Davis died," I pointed out. "And Gage told us that he saw another Were attack Nicholas. Maybe that Were killed its next victim."

"I think you're jumping to conclusions," Rose protested. "It could have been someone or something other than a werewolf that murdered Mr. Davis."

But I was still hung up on my Were theory. There were only two new people in town, as far as I knew: Elise Wilder and Duke Sherrad. Maybe it was one of them. Was Penny right about Duke? Was he just a charming fortune-teller? Or was Duke the mysterious new werewolf in town?

CHAPTER TEN

Two nights later, the Giordano family went to Mort's, along with what seemed like everyone else in Nightshade, for Mr. Davis's memorial service. It was rare that Mom got out of work so early, and I was a little sad that we couldn't spend the evening doing something fun together instead of hanging out at a funeral home. But I hoped I'd be able to pick up some clues at the service about Mr. Davis's mysterious death.

The Eternal Rest Room was packed. I drifted over to where Samantha was standing with a gaggle of weepy cheerleaders. I craned my neck to get a look at the casket over the crowd standing around it. It was closed. It seemed I wouldn't get a look at Mr. Davis's body after all.

A tiny woman wearing a lace veil stood in front of the casket, greeting mourners.

"Who's that?" I whispered to Sam.

"Mrs. Wilder. Matriarch of the Wilder clan. I met her when I booked the Wilder mansion for prom. Strange lady. Sweet, though."

I was confused. "Wilder?" I said. "Was she related to Mr. Davis?"

"Didn't you know?" Sam said. "Mr. Davis was Mrs. Wilder's grandson."

"That makes Elise and Mr. Davis cousins," I said.

"Duh, Daisy," hissed Penny, who was obviously listening in on our conversation. "Everybody knows that."

Sure enough, there was Elise at the front of the room, looking gorgeous even with red-rimmed eyes. I felt a little less sympathetic when I saw who she was talking to. Ryan.

"Excuse me," I mumbled, and pushed my way out into the hall. I could see Penny's gloating smile out of the corner of my eye.

I leaned against the wall and sighed deeply. Evidently there were others who needed a break from the service, too. There was a commotion in a little sitting room across the hall, but nobody else seemed to notice. It was Bane Paxton's parents, their youngest son, Wolfgang, and a beautiful woman I didn't recognize. She had shiny midnight black hair that hung long and straight, past her waist. She was petite but muscular-looking. I was drawn to the feeling of immense power she gave off in waves.

As I watched, Wolfgang started to shake, and a minute later hair sprouted all over his face, his jaw elongated, and sharp fangs jutted from his mouth.

"Wolfgang!" his mother said. "Please control yourself."

"He's so upset," his dad said to the raven-haired woman. "Mr. Davis was his favorite teacher."

The beautiful woman put a comforting hand on his arm. "He's young," she said in a soothing voice. "Controlling a shift takes years of practice. Let me talk to him." She threw her cloak over Wolfgang to hide his condition and led him out of the building.

I had no idea that the Paxtons were shape-shifters. Was the beautiful woman a shape-shifter too? She seemed to know what she was talking about when she spoke of shifting.

I heard someone calling my name from another doorway down the hall. It was Poppy summoning me to the Tranquility Room.

"I should have figured you'd be in here," I said. There was Gage, pacing in front of the fireplace.

"Gage just told me there was a Nightshade City Council meeting here last night," Poppy said excitedly. My ears perked up.

"Was it about Mr. Davis?" I asked.

Gage nodded. "They think they know who killed him. The Scourge."

I frowned. Who or what was the Scourge? Where had I heard that before? "Are you sure that's what they said? They didn't mention a werewolf?" I asked Gage.

Gage nodded resolutely. "I was there the whole time. The Skull with the gavel said the Scourge was involved."

I flopped down on a velvet-covered couch to think. So much for a spy on the inside. Gage's information wasn't much help. But he and Poppy weren't focused on the case anyway—they were flirting in the corner. I had to admit there was something appealing about Gage. He was still sexy, even though he was see-through.

The door inched open and Rose and Nicholas entered. "I noticed you two disappeared," Rose said. "I figured you must be here."

I could hear Elise's voice wafting from the Eternal Rest Room. I couldn't hear everything, but it was clear she was giving a speech about her cousin.

"I recognize that voice," Gage said. "The girl with the amber eyes. She was at the city council meeting." Poppy looked a little annoyed at Gage's wistful description. I didn't want to remind her that *she* shouldn't be the one jealous of Elise.

I sat up, eager to hear more. "So if the Wilders are part of the city council, that must mean there's something . . . different about them," I observed. I looked to Nicholas for confirmation.

"Yes, Daisy, the Wilders are shifters," he admitted.

"So Mr. Davis was a werewolf?"

He shook his head. "There are many kinds of shifters—wolves, big cats, even fluffy little bunnies."

Fluffy little bunnies? I swallowed a giggle.

"Well, do you think it was a Were that killed Mr. Davis?" Poppy asked, tactful as usual.

Nicholas looked stung. "No, in fact I know it wasn't," he said. "But whoever did it went to great lengths to make it look like a Were attack."

"How do you know?" I asked.

"I thoroughly inspected the body before my father prepared it for burial," Nicholas said. "Those marks were made by a human, probably using some sort of metal instrument to make it look like he was clawed. We Weres have excellent olfactory senses, you know." With that he swept out of the room.

"I hope we didn't offend Nicholas," Poppy said. Rose shot her a sharp look and followed after him.

I didn't feel like being a third wheel on Poppy's date with the dead, so I returned to the Eternal Rest Room, which was clearing out after the service. Ryan wasn't there. Neither was Elise.

My mom was still there, talking quietly with Chief Mendez. Were they flirting? It was hard to tell. "I'm telling you, Pete," I heard her saying as I got closer. "I can't help that. It's what I see. A cup. Nothing more."

The chief's brow was creased in concentration, but he snapped out of it and smiled when he saw me approaching.

"There you are, Daisy," Mom said. "Let's get going. Are your sisters coming?"

"I think they want to hang out here a little longer," I said.

We said good-bye to the chief. "Daisy, Ryan told me to tell you good night for him," he said. "He's sorry that he had to go without talking to you, but something came up."

I shrugged. What else was new?

In the car, Mom asked me if everything was okay with Ryan and me.

"He's avoiding me," I admitted. "Something's wrong, but I don't know what."

Mom looked sympathetic. "Oh, don't worry about it so much, Daisy," she said. "It's probably just temporary. A hormonal thing."

A hormonal thing? What was she talking about? It's not like guys had to worry about that time of the month. Besides, she of all people should understand why I have abandonment issues. I decided to change the subject.

"Mom, what's the Scourge?"

Her eyes widened and darted away from the road and onto me for a second. "What did you say?"

I repeated my question. Mom pulled into our driveway but left the car running. She seemed relieved not to be on the road anymore—obviously what I had said had her distracted, though I didn't know why.

"Daisy, how did you hear about the Scourge?" she asked in a shaky voice.

"Let's just say a ghost told me," I said.

Her expression was grave. "Don't joke around about them," she said. "They're very, very dangerous."

"Them?"

She hesitated a fraction of a second before explaining

more. "They're a group of people who have sworn to eradicate all paranormals."

"Eradicate? You mean . . ."

"Kill? Yes, that's exactly what I mean." She shut off the car engine and spoke to me in her most serious tone. "Daisy, I know you've got the makings of a great psychic detective. But this is way over your head. You do not want to get mixed up with the Scourge. They can make people disappear if they want to."

Disappear? Now who did that remind me of? I nodded, chilled by my mom's words. Sure enough, she was fiddling with her wedding ring. She only got this emotional when Dad was involved. But what was my father's connection to the Scourge?

"If you know something, please tell me," Mom said.

I wished, more than anything, that I had the answers she wanted. But the truth was, I was more confused than ever.

CHAPTER ELEVEN

Despite warnings from Mom and Chief Mendez not to get involved, I couldn't help myself. I had to find out what happened to Mr. Davis. I figured the best way to proceed would be to start where he started. So the next day after school, when Mom was still at work, I said to my sisters, "I'm going to go check out Mr. Davis's house. Want to come with me?"

Rose sighed, but she grabbed the keys. "Let's go," she said. I guess she figured coming with me was better than my going alone as soon as I could give her the slip.

Rose drove, Poppy rode shotgun, and I got stuck in the back.

One advantage to living in a town the size of Nightshade was that every girl in school who had even a slight crush on Mr. Davis had gushed about his house, a quaint little cottage on Hart Street, which meant that I didn't have to try to get his address. It wasn't as if any student had actually made it inside his place, because Mr. Davis was always proper and aboveboard about that sort of thing, but many a lovesick girl had driven past his house night after night.

We parked around the corner and walked as casually as possible down his street. The air was still and hot, and there was nobody around.

The cottage reminded me of something out of a Beatrix Potter book, complete with a picket fence and roses on a trellis. Several flowering bushes with pink blooms framed his front door. I half expected to see Peter sneaking into Mr. McGregor's field, but all I saw was a small vegetable garden with no sign of the famous rabbit.

The police had obviously been here before us, judging from all the yellow and black crime-scene tape. Part of me was relieved that they'd already been through and swept the place for clues, but part of me worried that there wouldn't be anything left for me.

"Let's go around back," I suggested. "Maybe there's a door that can't be seen from the street."

"How are we going to get in?" Rose wanted to know. "We shouldn't leave any fingerprints."

Good question. We both looked at Poppy, who grinned.

"Okay," she said, "but if we get caught, it was already unlocked."

She stared at the door, her forehead wrinkling only a second, and then the door flew open.

We stepped inside gingerly, careful not to touch anything.

The cottage was just four rooms: a kitchen, a small dining room, a living room that evidently had also served as Mr.

Davis's bedroom, and a bathroom so tiny that the three of us could barely fit in there at once.

"What are we looking for?" Rose asked.

"A clue. Something out of place," I said.

We checked the kitchen first. My powers weren't under control enough for me to try to use them at a crime scene, so Poppy had to use her powers to open every cupboard in the room. Once she finished, she wandered into the dining room.

"That china is beautiful, and it has to be over a hundred years old," Rose exclaimed. "Too bad there's a missing piece."

"Look at all these pictures," Poppy called from the living room/bedroom.

Rose and I moved to where Poppy stood in front of a wall of framed photographs.

There were several photos of Mr. Davis with Elise Wilder, Mrs. Wilder (I almost didn't recognize her without the black veil), and other family members.

"Mr. Davis was in drama club," Rose said.

I looked over to where she was pointing. In it, a younger Mr. Davis wore a suit and tons of stage makeup, and he stood next to three other guys. One of them looked familiar, although I couldn't place him. He had blond hair and thick black glasses.

"He looks so young," I observed.

Rose agreed. "Nice costumes, though."

"*Arsenic and Old Lace*," Poppy commented.

"How do you know that?" I asked.

"I dated Sam Tsai, the drama king, for three weeks during last spring's production. Penny Edwards played one of the little old ladies. Don't you pay attention to anything that goes on at school?"

"I must have missed Penny's stellar performance," I said. My sarcasm was lost on my sister. "He must have gone to an all-guys school," I commented, since the cast of this production appeared to be exclusively male. I peered closer. There was something familiar about the guy in the photo, the one with glasses and the case of bad acne that showed even through his makeup.

"It looks like a private school," Rose said. "Charles Fey College." She pointed to an orange and navy scarf that was draped over a chair and was stamped with the school name.

I noticed a leather-bound date book on the desk below the photos. Hoping I wouldn't mess up and break anything, I picked it up telekinetically and flipped to the date Mr. Davis had died. He had jotted, "Tea with HH."

"These Wilders sure love their tea," I observed. "Samantha mentioned to me there's a tearoom at the mansion."

"I wonder who HH is," Rose said as the datebook wobbled from side to side as it hovered in front of her. "I can't think of anyone in Nightshade with those initials."

"Maybe it was a date," said Poppy.

Our discussion was interrupted when we heard a car pull up and a door slam. I dropped the datebook and froze as I heard the click of high heels coming up the walkway.

I couldn't resist a peek through the peephole. Elise Wilder was only feet from the front door. She stopped and sniffed the air. Her nose twitched as if she smelled something bad. I jumped back. I could have sworn that her strange yellowish eyes could see me through the heavy oak door.

"We've got to get out of here," I whispered.

Poppy and Rose nodded to signal that they understood, and then as quietly as possible, we went through the back door. We broke into a jog and didn't stop running until we'd reached the car and pulled away.

"That was close," Poppy said.

"I wonder what Elise was doing there," I said.

"He *was* her cousin," Rose said. "She was probably just checking to make sure the cottage wasn't totally trashed after the police left."

"Oh no!" Poppy said.

"What?" Rose and I exclaimed together.

"I didn't have a chance to shut the cupboards. They're still wide open."

"Maybe Elise will think the police left it that way," I reassured her.

"I hope so," she replied.

But that night, I dreamed I was a frightened rabbit being chased through a forest by Elise, who had morphed into a killingly beautiful wolf.

CHAPTER TWELVE

The next day at school, I yawned my way through my classes.

At the prom committee meeting after school, Samantha reminded me that I still had to apply for the permit to have the after party in the park, so I stopped by the police station on my way home and talked to Chief Mendez.

"Are you sure the park is the best place for the party?" he asked, looking over the application.

"Why not?" I said. "You said yourself that the citizens of Nightshade are perfectly safe. And I'm sure you'll have your investigation into Mr. Davis's murder all squared away by the time prom rolls around."

Chief Mendez smiled. "You're right, Daisy," he said, but his smile seemed forced. "Even so, I'll put some extra officers on duty in the park that night."

He handed me our approved permit for the party.

It was getting dark by the time I headed home, but I decided to cut through the park anyway. I wanted to check out the layout and try to envision how we would set things up on prom night. Plus, maybe I'd find something to give me a clue about Mr. Davis.

I walked to the fountain at the center of the park. The diamond in the crown.

I avoided a dark splotch on the path near the fountain. It looked like blood. I bent down to examine the area. It turned out to be nothing more than melted chocolate from an ice-cream cone. Gross. I was about to get up when I spotted a couple on a bench several feet away from me.

I saw the back of a tall guy's head. It was Ryan, sitting with Elise. They were engrossed in conversation and didn't notice me.

The tight, miserable feeling in my chest didn't leave me. My legs were shaky, so I sat down on the ground and leaned against the fountain. The last time I'd had this sensation had been in sixth grade, when Kyle Vendajas, a boy I had a mad crush on, picked me last in dodgeball.

I put my head down on the cold, smooth surface of the fountain and just sat there. I wanted to cry, but forced the tears back. I don't know how long I stayed like that, but when I finally looked again, they were gone. Who was Elise to Ryan, and why had he been spending so much time with her?

It was getting darker, and I needed to get home. Ever since Mr. Davis's murder, rumors had been flying around about wolves roaming the park in packs.

When I stood up, I felt a tingle and I realized my foot was asleep. I stomped it once to get the circulation going, and that's when I heard a noise coming from the bushes. I moved closer.

Meow. A tiny face peered out of the leaves. A black kitten stared up at me, still meowing plaintively. She took a hesitant step forward and then batted something toward me. It was a bit of greenery covered with pink blossoms. I knew some plants were harmful to animals, so I took it away from her and put it in my pocket.

She seemed miffed at being deprived of her plaything and let out a plaintive meow.

The kitten wasn't wearing a collar. I inched closer, not wanting to startle her. She edged back toward the shelter of the bush.

I looked at the darkening sky. Definitely time to head home, but I couldn't just leave her there. I remembered that the remains of my lunch were stuffed into my backpack. I hadn't felt much like eating, and the bell had rung before I could dump it.

I dug through my pack and found the untouched roast beef sandwich. I gutted the sandwich and waved a slice of meat in front of her enticingly. Somehow I was sure the kitten was a she.

"Here, kitty, kitty."

She moved forward cautiously. I dropped the roast beef a

few feet in front of her and then stepped back. Cats didn't like to be crowded, I knew. Or picked up by strangers. I didn't relish getting scratched, but if the roast beef didn't work, I'd have to grab her and scoot out of the park.

The kitten used a claw to hook the meat and drag it closer to herself. I dropped another, smaller piece a few feet down the path. She froze and stared at me with huge sapphire eyes. At this rate, we'd be here all night.

I tried again. She inched forward slowly, on her belly. I dropped a tiny piece of roast beef for her every few feet. I thought she'd gulp it down, but instead she ate daintily.

When she was through, she meowed again, as if to say "More, please." She wound herself around my legs. We'd become friends, but we'd run out of time. I heard a far-off howl. "Time to leave, kitten."

I took off at a brisk pace. The howling grew closer. The kitten bristled, all her fur standing on end, and then trotted after me.

I wondered exactly how many werewolves there were in Nightshade. I didn't want to find out tonight. Evidently, neither did the kitten. We practically ran the rest of the way home.

I didn't stop until we reached the white picket fence that enclosed our yard. I opened the gate. "Are you coming in?" I asked.

The kitten walked through the gate with a swish of her

tail. She paused on the front porch and meowed. Suddenly, I had a cat, or she had me.

I wondered what Mom would say about having a pet. I unlocked the door and opened it wide. The cat entered with the regal walk of a queen deigning to receive her subjects.

"Guess what I found today?" I called out. No time like the present to find out Mom's current stance on pets.

There was no answer.

"Poppy? Mom? Rose?" I checked my watch. It was past seven. Where was everyone? "It looks like it's just you and me, kitten."

We didn't have any cat food, of course, so I opened a can of tuna. Who knew how long it had been since the kitten had had a good meal? She was more than sleek, she was skinny. I would take her to the vet as soon as I could, but in the meantime I needed to run to the store for cat food and a litter box, maybe even a few cat toys, but I didn't want to leave my new friend alone.

The phone rang while I was watching the cat eat. I checked the caller ID but didn't recognize the number.

"Hello?" I said. I was hoping it was Ryan. It wasn't.

"May I speak to Daizee?"

It was Duke Sherrad. I could tell by the way he kind of stretched out my name when he said it.

"Hi, Duke."

"You recognized me." He sounded pleased.

It didn't take a detective to figure it out. No one else in Nightshade had that accent. "What's up?"

"What is up?" Now he sounded puzzled. He had to be playing, right?

I'd forgotten Duke might not be familiar with some slang. Where exactly was he from, anyway?

I tried again. "I was just asking why you were calling." I was waiting for him to get to the point, but he seemed to be taking his time.

"I was calling to ask you if you would do me the honor of accompanying me to the upcoming ball?" He sounded really nervous now, and I took pity on him.

"The ball? You mean *prom*?"

"Yes, yes. This is it. The prom. Penny Edwards indicated that I would require formal wear. I have a tuxedo already."

Somehow I doubted that Penny was encouraging Duke to ask me out. "Does Penny know you are asking me to prom?"

"Why, no. Should I have informed her of this?"

"No, of course not. I was just curious." Penny was definitely interested in Duke. If she thought I was competition, there's no telling what she was capable of doing.

"You will go with me, yes?"

I'd never been in the position of letting someone down, gently or otherwise. Where was Poppy when I needed her? I gave the cat an entreating look, but she just licked a bit of tuna off her face. "You're no help," I whispered.

"I am afraid I did not hear what you said," Duke responded.

"It wasn't important," I said. I took a deep breath. "Duke, I'm flattered, and under other circumstances, I'd be delighted to go with you, but I'm already seeing someone."

"This Ryan you introduced to me?"

"Yes."

"And he has already asked you to this prom?"

"Not yet," I said. My mind flashed to a picture of Ryan and Elise huddled together on the park bench. "But he will," I said, with more confidence than I was feeling.

"If he does not extend an invitation, I would be happy to escort you," Duke said.

"Thank you, Duke, but that won't be necessary." At least I hoped it wouldn't.

After a few more fulsome compliments, Duke finally hung up. I caught myself smiling at the phone. I have to admit my ego was soothed by his obvious interest.

My family still wasn't home, so I scrounged leftovers for dinner, then remembered I still needed cat supplies. Poppy had the car, so I'd have to ask her to stop on her way home.

I dialed her cell, but it went right to voice mail. "Hey, where are you?" I said. "Can you stop at the store and pick up a litter box and some cat litter? I'll explain later."

After I hung up the phone, I grabbed Mom's old copy of *The Big Book of Fortune-Telling* and curled up on the couch. The kitten jumped up and purred approvingly before settling in next to me.

I became engrossed in my reading and lost track of the time. I raised my head only when I heard a car pulling into the driveway.

Poppy rushed in with a huge smile on her face. "Daisy? Where are you?" She was carrying a huge bag of cat litter, so I knew she'd gotten my message.

"Thanks for stopping at the store," I said. I gestured toward the kitten. "Look who I found tonight. Think Mom will let us keep her?"

"Oh, she's adorable, how could Mom refuse?" Poppy said. "There's another bag of stuff in the car."

"I'll get it."

I left Poppy and the kitten playing happily.

I was half in and half out of the car, rummaging around in the back seat for the bag Poppy had mentioned, when I got the feeling someone was watching me.

"Is someone there?"

There wasn't an answer, but I could hear someone breathing.

I grabbed the bag, slammed the car door, and headed for my front porch. A figure stepped out of the shadows.

"I didn't mean to scare you. It's me."

I recognized the voice and stopped in my tracks. "Ryan, you scared me half to death. What are you doing here?"

"I'm sorry," he said. "I just wanted to talk to you. Here, let me carry that." I handed him the litter box.

He stared at it, puzzled. "I didn't know you had a cat."

"Well, a lot can happen in a few days." My voice was arctic in its chilliness. I stomped up the steps.

He trailed after me uncertainly. I opened the door and he hesitated.

"You may as well come in." I didn't look behind me to see if he was coming.

"Hi, Ryan," Poppy said.

He put down the cat box and sat on the couch. The kitten, traitor that she was, immediately jumped into his lap and began to purr.

I didn't meet his eyes, but instead spent a few minutes checking out everything Poppy had bought. Cat food, litter, a couple of toys, even an adorable cat bed. She'd thought of everything.

"Where'd you get her?" Ryan said. At least, that's what he said out loud. But I heard his thoughts, which were jumbled and chaotic. *I can't tell her the truth.*

My powers seemed to always tune in at the worst possible time. I glared at him.

Poppy yawned widely and unconvincingly. "Time for me

and the kitten to head for bed." She stood, and the kitten jumped down from Ryan's lap.

I didn't say anything after she left the room. I was still trying to process what I'd heard.

I tried to focus on his thoughts again, but all I got was a jumbled mess.

"The cat? Where'd you get her?" Ryan repeated.

"I found her in the park tonight," I said, watching him closely to see if he squirmed.

He did. Deeply.

CHAPTER THIRTEEN

We sat staring at each other for a moment. I cleared my throat. "Where were you tonight?" I tried to sound casual, but it came out like an accusation.

"Why do you want to know?" Ryan asked. He stared at his hands.

I was sick of the games. "Where were you last weekend? And why have you been avoiding me?"

He didn't know what to say, what lies to tell me.

"Ryan, just tell me the truth. I can take it."

His thought jumped into my mind. *No, you can't.*

It was as bad as I had anticipated. He was going to dump me for that girl. I braced myself for the breakup, but it never came.

"I can't tell you right now, Daisy. It's . . . complicated." His hands were shaking.

"Then tell me what's going on between you and Elise Wilder," I said.

"I can't tell you that, either," he replied. "Daisy, you have to trust me, I—"

"I don't have to do anything," I snapped. "It's late. I think it's time you went home."

Ryan didn't argue, which, although it was completely illogical, upset me even more.

I walked him to the door. He didn't try to kiss me.

After he left, I leaned back against the door and tried to still my whirling thoughts. What was going on in Nightshade? Why would anyone want to hurt Mr. Davis? And most importantly, what was going on with Ryan?

Poppy came galloping down the stairs seconds later. "What was that all about?" she asked.

From her tone of voice, it was clear that she had probably been perched at the top of the stairs, listening the whole time.

"Nothing," I muttered. I sat down on the couch and turned on the TV with the volume up loud to avoid any further conversation with my busybody sister. Poppy shrugged and flopped down on the couch next to me.

Our eyes were glued to the tube when Mom came home. Time to break the news about my new pet. There were deep lines on her face, and she was frowning. Maybe not the best time to introduce the topic.

"Mom, I found a kitten tonight. Can I keep her?"

Her expression softened. "A pet is a lot of responsibility," she said. "You can't just go haring off whenever it pleases you. A kitten needs attention and care. And what's going to happen to it when you leave for college?"

Poppy and I exchanged looks. "We're sorry, Mom," she said.

"Yeah, but I just couldn't leave her in the park," I said.

"I'm not changing the litter box, and you girls have to feed her in the morning before school."

"Does that mean we can keep her?" I asked.

As if on cue, the kitten strolled into the room, looking completely adorable.

"Mom, please?" Poppy said. "She's so cute!"

"We'll take care of her," I said. "I promise."

"Well, okay," Mom said. "Since your birthday is coming up, I suppose you can keep her. Consider this an early birthday present."

"Thanks, Mom!" I reached down and picked up the kitten, thrilled that she would be staying with us after all.

"You've got to give her a name, Daisy," Poppy said. "We can't keep calling her 'kitten' forever."

I studied the cat for a moment. "I'll call her Midnight." I cradled my kitten in my arms, glad to have a new little friend to comfort me, especially since things seemed to be going down the tubes with me and Ryan. But something Mom had said gave me a faint glimmer of hope. My birthday was only days away. Maybe Ryan would surprise me. Maybe things could be turned around after all. Seventeen was a brand new year.

CHAPTER FOURTEEN

When the big day arrived, I was greeted at my locker by Samantha, who held a big balloon bouquet. I was touched that she had remembered.

"Thanks, Sam!" I said. "You're the first one to wish me a happy birthday."

"That's just sad," she said. "What about your sisters? Your mom?"

"Oh, besides them," I said. "We all went out for a birthday breakfast at Slim's. And we're celebrating with Grandma Giordano this weekend."

"And Ryan?"

I looked away. "I haven't talked to him."

Sam didn't say anything, but we were both thinking the same thing. What kind of boyfriend doesn't even remember his own girlfriend's birthday?

"How about if we celebrate tonight?" Sam suggested. "We can check out the restaurant in the Wilder mansion."

I gave her a look of disgust. "Going to Elise Wilder's house isn't exactly my idea of a happy birthday."

"Oh, I'm sure she'll be holed up in her private quarters," Sam said. "She's not very social, in case you haven't noticed."

She seemed plenty sociable with Ryan.

"Come on," Sam pleaded, "I've got to go up there to approve the final menu for prom, anyway. I stretched the entertainment budget to include a few munchies. We're going there to sample the food."

I finally agreed. Maybe I could find out more about my rival.

Sean walked up as we were talking and wrapped his arms around Samantha. "Can I come with?"

"You can tag along as long as you remember your manners," Sam said.

Sean waved at Ryan, who was walking down the hall. "Hey, bro, wait up. Wanna go to dinner with our ladies?"

Inwardly, I wanted to kill Sean. It was clear that Ryan couldn't stand to be in the same room with me. I certainly wasn't his "lady" now, if I'd ever been.

Ryan skulked back to where we stood. "Where are you going?" Still no eye contact. He had dark circles under his eyes and looked like he hadn't had a shower in the last few days. He didn't seem to notice the balloons I held.

"That Wilder place," Sean replied.

"I'll meet you there," Ryan said, and walked away.

Samantha looked me up and down. I had to present a class project that morning, so I was more dressed up than normal, which meant instead of my usual jeans, I was actually wearing a skirt. Which meant I passed (judging from her expression, barely) Sam's standards of appropriate dinner attire.

After school, Sam drove us to Sean's, and the two of us waited in the car while Sean went inside to change.

"Have you decided yet?" she asked me the second Sean was inside his house.

"Decided what?"

"If you're going to keep waiting for Ryan to ask you to prom or if you're going to take Duke up on his offer."

"Like Duke's hanging around waiting for *me*." I didn't want to admit that I was still over the moon for Ryan, even though lately he was acting like he'd forgotten I existed.

Samantha raised an eyebrow and gave me a look.

I finally understood her unspoken message. "He can't be," I said. "Girls are lining up for the chance to date Duke Sherrad, gypsy fortune-teller and hottie."

"He hasn't asked anybody else," she said. "Plenty of private readings with the competition, though."

Somehow, I didn't like the idea of Duke alone with someone else. "What about Ryan?" I protested.

"What about him?" she said. "He has to know by now that prom is coming up. You need to remind him that you have options, too."

The conversation ended when Sean returned, but it lingered in my mind on the ride over. What did Sam mean by her "options, *too*" comment? Was Ryan exploring other options? It certainly looked like it. Was it truly over for Ryan and me? Should I give Duke a chance?

When the mansion came into view, I held back a gasp. It was gorgeous. It looked like a medieval castle, complete with creeping ivy and stone walls.

The inside of the Wilder mansion was also breathtaking, positively dripping Old World elegance. Great, the competition was not only gorgeous; she was loaded. Not that money and power mattered to Ryan, but I did feel slightly intimidated.

We waited in the lobby until a dark-haired woman in a severely cut black dress led us to our table. It wasn't until we sat down that I realized she was the woman I'd noticed with the Paxtons at Mr. Davis's memorial service.

She smiled at me. "Enjoy your meal, Daisy." I checked her name tag. It read bianca. The mystery shifter's name was Bianca.

We were seated at a lovely table overlooking the garden. Faded pink roses climbed the wallpaper, and real crystal shone on the crisp linens covering the table. I noticed that all the utensils were made of gold. Werewolves hated silver. Silver bullets and all that.

Samantha stared at Sean until he pulled out a chair for her.

He started to take his seat but then remembered to pull my chair out, too, since Ryan still hadn't shown.

We waited almost half an hour, but he didn't appear.

"He's not coming," I said glumly. "We may as well order." I was trying not to cry, but despite everything, I didn't think Ryan would forget my birthday.

Sean motioned to the discreetly hovering server and we ordered.

The service was excellent, the food delicious, but I could have been eating my English lit essay for all I tasted it.

Ryan's not showing on my birthday was a sign that our relationship was ending. I never thought of myself as the kind of girl who sat around waiting for some guy to ask her to prom—heck, a few months ago, prom and Ryan Mendez both seemed out of reach—but here I was, waiting.

And I was sick of it.

"I'm going to take a walk," I said as the server cleared our plates. "I won't be long."

Bianca said, "There's a hedge maze at the rear of the garden. It's one of our most popular attractions and dates back over a hundred years." She pointed to the French doors. "It's right through there."

I noticed there was a pamphlet display case full of maps of the maze, but I ignored it. I was too angry to stop.

I went through the double doors and spotted the maze at

the far end of the garden. The Wilder house's gardens were extensive, and any other time I might have stopped to enjoy the smell of jasmine and honeysuckle. I also noticed bushes covered with pink flowers, but I didn't know what they were called. They were the same kind that grew around Mr. Davis's cottage.

The longer I walked, the madder I got about Ryan's no-show. By the time I entered the hedge maze, I was steamed. What was going on with him? And how much longer did he expect me to put up with it without an explanation?

The night air cooled my overheated skin. The moon illuminated the path through the high, manicured hedges but concealed as much as it revealed.

A dog barked in the distance and was answered by a low growling sound. The noise sent a shiver through me. Why had I come out here alone? Why hadn't I taken a map of the maze? I didn't have the greatest sense of direction, something I'd neglected to consider when I set out.

Something rustled in the bushes and I jumped, but it was only a harmless rabbit. It was as scared of me as I had been of it, and it scurried off down the opposite path. I walked on, determined to make my way out of the maze.

I turned left and then left again, pausing when I thought I heard something. A minute later, I heard a low growling and I froze, straining to hear it again, but the only sound was the mournful sigh of the wind.

I made a right turn and came to a dead end. There was someone behind me, breathing softly, but I didn't want to turn around. I was trapped. After an agonizing minute, I whirled around and saw a huge, slavering beast. I had seen a creature like this once before, at a Nightshade City Council meeting. There was no mistaking it for a normal wolf. My mind processed that I was looking at a werewolf, and this time, not from a safe distance. It put its head down and made a whimpering sound before turning and trotting off down the path to the left.

Panic overtaking me, I ran down the opposite path, mindlessly following the twists and turns of the maze. When I finally reached the exit, winded and sweating, the beast had vanished.

CHAPTER FIFTEEN

When I got home, the house was quiet. I called to Midnight, but she was nowhere to be found. She was probably sulking in a corner somewhere because I hadn't been home to give her her kibble. I felt a little guilty.

I jumped when I saw Nicholas Bone sitting at our kitchen counter.

"Hi, Nicholas," I said cautiously. "Where's Rose?" I tried not to make it obvious that I was inching toward the spot where the calendar hung. I wanted to check the moon's cycle, as he tended to turn rather furry during a full moon, and I wasn't looking forward to a repeat performance of my encounter in the maze.

"She's changing," he said. "We're heading to the Black Opal later."

He noticed what I was doing and cleared his throat. Who says werewolves are all bark and no brains? "There was just a full moon a couple weeks ago, Daisy. Remember?"

Embarrassed, I looked over at him.

Nicholas had his arm in a sling, and it was also wrapped in what looked like about a million bandages from the incident on the night of the last full moon. It looked like a lot more than a little bitty accident, and I wondered why Rose had downplayed his injuries.

"Sorry," I said, feeling silly for panicking. I paused before sheepishly asking, "How does it work, exactly?"

Nicholas stared at me in amusement. "Being a werewolf?"

I nodded. "Is it possible for them to shift even if it's not a full moon?"

Nicholas sighed and looked down at his injured arm, as if reliving painful memories. "When you're young—when the gift first manifests—it's nearly impossible to control. It can happen anytime."

I recalled Wolfgang Paxton's spontaneous wolf-out at the memorial service. "It must be scary to have that overtake you when you least expect it," I said.

"It is," Nicholas said. "But it gets easier as time goes on. As a fully mature Were, I only shift during the full moon. It took lots of training, but I can control the beast within me."

I thought about it. I really was ignorant about what it meant to be a Were. I wouldn't make that mistake again. I knew how I felt when people treated me differently. First when I was the only norm in the family, and then when I got my powers.

"I think I know what you mean." At his look of surprise, I

continued. "It's like with my powers. I can't always control them. Sometimes they control me. But I'm working at it, and I'm getting better at making them do what I want to do, instead of the opposite." I paused for a moment, chewing on what he had told me. "So I guess the Were I saw tonight must have been a youngster."

Nicholas's eyes widened. "You saw a Were tonight? Where?"

I explained what happened in the hedge maze at the Wilder mansion. "Do you think it could have been Elise?" I asked.

"Hard to say," Nicholas said cryptically. "Whoever it was, I wouldn't worry too much. They obviously didn't intend any harm."

"Yeah, I guess I got off easy," I said, gesturing toward his arm.

Suddenly Nicholas sniffed at the air. "What's that smell? It's coming from you."

"Thanks a lot," I mumbled. I wasn't wearing any perfume, so I wasn't sure what odor he could be referring to.

"Check your pockets," Nicholas said, zeroing in on the source.

I was wearing the same jacket I had worn to the park a few nights ago. I hunted through the pockets and pulled out the shriveled plant Midnight had been playing with when I found her.

He took it from me and sniffed it. "I can smell oleander, mixed with a faint hint of M&Ms."

"Oleander? Isn't that poisonous?" It was a good thing I had taken it away from my kitten.

"You should be careful with that," Nicholas warned. "Oleander *is* poisonous, but you can find it almost anywhere. Where did you pick this up?"

"Right by the fountain in the park. Where they found Mr. Davis's body."

A niggling thought was forming at the back of my mind. Could this oleander be somehow related to Mr. Davis's death? I couldn't figure out how to tie it to the murder, except that I'd found it in the same location.

Rose swept into the room, wearing a sparkly orchid-colored tank top perfect for clubbing.

"Tell Mom I won't be back until late, okay, Daisy?" she said. She winked and gave a little nod toward Nicholas. That's when I realized that her lips hadn't moved. I still wasn't totally used to the whole telepathic thing. I was used to Rose being able to read my mind, but not the other way around. And I blushed bright red when I realized where, exactly, her mind was. I did not need to have an image of that in my brain.

I headed to bed, but I couldn't sleep. I was too wound up with the thought that a volatile werewolf was on the loose in Nightshade. I shuddered as I remembered its eerie eyes and huge teeth.

There was a loud bang as an object hit my bedroom window. I jumped and then peered out.

Ryan stood below my window. "Daisy, come outside. I need to talk to you," he said in a carrying whisper.

I held up my hand and said, "I'll be right down." But before I did, I took a look at myself in the mirror. Frizzy hair, pale face, and ratty old pjs. Not exactly the image I wanted Ryan to carry with him, even if I was mad at him.

I quickly put on a cute hoodie over my faded boy-band T-shirt and put my hair into a ponytail. I added a little lip gloss and then scampered down the stairs as quietly as I could. I snagged a breath mint out of my purse in the hallway, where I'd thrown it earlier.

"Hey," Ryan said. He was sitting in the swing on the front porch. "I'm sorry I didn't make it to your birthday dinner. Something came up." I was about to roll my eyes after having to hear yet another one of his excuses when he held out a small, brightly wrapped package.

I sat next to him and opened the present. It was a gold locket. It looked old.

"It was my mom's," he said.

"Ryan . . ."

"I want you to have it. She used to say it would protect her from harm. Will you please wear it?"

And then I was in his arms and he was kissing me like his life depended on it. He didn't stop kissing me until we were both hot and sweaty and way too overheated.

Somehow, I'd ended up on my back, pressed against the seat of the swing. I put out a hand to his chest to slow things down, but I only had time to gulp in some air before Ryan bent toward me and nipped my lips, hard enough that he drew a little blood.

"Hey, watch it!" I said. He'd never done that before. It hadn't really hurt, but it had startled me.

Ryan sat up, breathing heavily. "Daisy, I'm sorry. I . . . I don't know what's gotten into me lately."

"What's going on with you? It seems like I never see you anymore, but then you show up here"—I looked at my watch—"at midnight."

"I wanted to talk to you," he said in a low voice. "I didn't mean to hurt you."

"It's okay," I said, trying not to let him know that I was blushing. "I was startled, that's all. I'm glad you're here. I wanted to talk to you, too."

"What did you want to talk to me about?"

About a million things. Elise, where he'd been lately, the werewolf. Where to start?

"Did your dad hear anything new about Mr. Davis?" I began. It seemed like the easiest place to start a conversation, but I was wrong about that.

Ryan tensed and looked away. "What about him?"

"Well, have the autopsy results come back yet?"

"I don't know," he replied tersely.

I sighed. "Well, until they do, I guess we won't know what killed him."

"It wasn't a werewolf, if that's what you're thinking," he said in a snotty tone of voice.

Why was he so defensive? Was it because his precious Elise was a shifter? "I didn't think so before, but now I have my doubts."

"What do you mean?" he snapped.

What was wrong with him? I couldn't even talk to him anymore. "Christy's mom saw claw marks on Mr. Davis's face." I ignored the fact that Nicholas had already confirmed that a human had made the marks. I had no reason to doubt Nicholas, but somehow, my mouth just wouldn't stop.

"Since when do you listen to gossip?" His voice was shaking with anger.

"It's not just that," I said. "The other night in the park, I heard howling. And just tonight, I came face-to-face with a werewolf!"

He stood so suddenly that he set the swing rocking furiously. "Do you know anything about werewolves? Their strength and speed? You could get hurt."

"Ryan, why are you so mad?"

He didn't answer at first. "This was a mistake. I've got to go."

"Ryan—" But he was already letting himself out of the front gate.

"Just let it go, Daisy," he called over his shoulder. "Let my dad handle the investigation." Then he ran down the street and disappeared into the darkness.

What just happened? I was baffled by Ryan's behavior. He couldn't deny that there was a werewolf on the loose in Nightshade. And even though I liked Nicholas and Chief Mendez, they had connections to the Nightshade City Council—and they could be covering up for the killer. No matter what Ryan said, I wasn't butting out of this investigation. Not a chance.

CHAPTER SIXTEEN

I was glad to spend the rest of the weekend away from Nightshade, at Grandma Giordano's place. But my troubles were still waiting for me when I got back. On Monday, Samantha found me during morning break.

She was with Jordan Kelley, a cheerleader who was definitely more Sam's friend than mine. Jordan was all right, but I didn't really see what Sam saw in her. Jordan probably wondered the same thing about me.

"So did you and Ryan make up yet?" Sam asked.

I glanced over at Jordan. She was nice enough, but I didn't feel like confiding my troubles to the entire school. "I don't want to talk about it."

Samantha said, "Jordan, why don't you go on along. I'll catch up with you later."

After Jordan left, there was silence.

"Honestly, I can't believe you two are still fighting," she said.

"You can't?" I asked incredulously. "Sam, you were there. He stood me up. On my birthday!"

"You mean he hasn't even tried to explain?"

"I'm getting mixed signals," I admitted, fiddling with the necklace he gave me. "He came over and gave me this the other night. Late."

"I can't believe he thought he could just drop in for a late-night booty call—"

"It wasn't like that, Sam," I said. "And since when do you use words like 'booty call'?"

"All I know is that he was majorly bummed all weekend. Sean told me he said he tried to talk to you, but you wouldn't listen. He's devastated."

"I find that hard to believe," I said. "After the way he acted the other night, it didn't seem like he even wanted to be with me anymore."

"That's ridiculous," Samantha said. "Even if he's been acting weird lately, Ryan Mendez is still totally in love with you. That's what he told Sean. Now, do you want to fix things or what?"

I nodded weakly. Of course I wanted to fix things. I just didn't know how.

"Why don't you come to their baseball game with me tonight? Then the four of us can go to Slim's afterward."

Despite my misgivings, I agreed to go.

"Great," she said. "I'll come over after school to get ready."

After school, we headed for Samantha's car. Instead of her BMW, she got into an older-model red VW convertible. Although still spiffy, it was a step down for a Devereaux.

"Where's the Beamer?" When had Samantha traded in her car? Her parents had just bought her the BMW less than a year ago.

She shrugged. "I got tired of it. This is cute, though, right?"

"Very cute, but—"

"It gets better gas mileage, too," she added.

I stared at her. Since when did Samantha care about saving gas? I narrowed my eyes at her. Something wasn't right.

The Sam I knew wouldn't be caught dead in a used car. I remembered the stack of past-due bills I'd found at her house a few months ago, but I decided not to say anything. It wasn't my business if the Devereauxs were having money troubles. I just hoped Sam would come to me when she needed someone to talk to. I didn't care about her money, or lack thereof, but I did care about Sam.

"What? I'm just trying to be a little more environmentally conscious. You should try it sometime," she said edgily.

Walking, which is what I did most of the time, was pretty much as environmentally conscious as you could get, but I wasn't going to say anything to Sam.

"I love the color," I said and then changed the subject. "What should I wear tonight?"

"Something that'll knock his cleats right off him," she said.

Samantha chattered away on the drive, but I only listened with half an ear. I was nervous about seeing Ryan.

At my house, Samantha vetoed half my closet before she found a midnight blue top I'd inherited from Poppy.

"This is more like it," she said.

I'd never worn it, because it showed more skin than I was used to showing. "I don't know," I said.

"Now let's find a skirt to show off those long legs of yours," she said.

"No skirt," I said. "It's freezing outside." A slight exaggeration, but it was overcast and windy.

"Okay," she said, "But no baggy jeans."

A thought struck me. "What if the game gets rained out?"

"It won't," she assured me. "Now hurry up and get dressed."

I was ready a few minutes later. I brushed off Samantha's attempts to do something with my hair. "Let's go! If we primp any longer, we'll miss the game."

When we got there, the field was damp. Our feet made squishing noises as we walked, and I was glad I'd opted for boots instead of skimpy sandals like the ones Samantha wore.

"You've got your gym sneakers in the car, right? Maybe you should grab them so your feet don't get soaked," I suggested to an uncomfortable-looking Sam.

"No thanks," she sniffed. "I want Sean to notice me, not think I'm one of his teammates."

"No chance of that," I said.

We found an open spot on the bleachers, and Samantha spread out a blanket to cover the cold metal bench.

The team was still warming up. My heart lurched when I saw Ryan in his uniform.

The school mascot was there, jumping around and generally making himself a nuisance. We were the Nightshade Sea Monsters, or Monsters for short.

A few minutes later Sean, concealed head to toe in catcher's gear, stepped behind the plate, and Ryan stepped up to the pitcher's mound and started to warm up.

Samantha gossiped with a couple of the girls from school, but I couldn't take my eyes off Ryan.

The game went by in a blur. I heard the crowd cheering, saw the teams take their turns at batting and fielding, but if you had asked me the score, I would have had no idea. I was mesmerized by the beauty of Ryan's body in motion.

Could I trust him? I hoped I could, but he was definitely keeping something from me. I hoped it wasn't another girlfriend.

It was a good thing my powers were so completely unreliable or I'd be tempted to peek into his mind to find out what he was hiding. Rose wouldn't approve, I know.

When the game was finally over and the teams had shaken hands, Ryan and Sean gathered up their gear and headed toward the bleachers where we were sitting.

"C'mon, let's go," Samantha said.

I stared at her, puzzled. We were going to leave without talking to the guys?

She explained, "I want Sean to get the full effect of my outfit. They'll catch up." If she didn't catch pneumonia first.

Samantha and I grabbed our stuff and headed for the snack bar. They jogged up to us by a picnic table.

"Daisy, you made it!" Ryan said. He wrapped his arms around me, and I leaned in and touched my lips to the cinnamon-colored skin near his neck. He jumped as if shocked by the contact and then pulled me closer for a kiss. Maybe Sam was right and everything was going to be okay after all.

"We're heading to the diner," Sean said. "Do you guys want to come with?"

Ryan bent down and whispered in my ear, his breath tickling my neck. "I'd rather be alone with you. My dad's working late tonight."

"I think we'll pass," I said.

We walked with Samantha and Sean to the parking lot. After they left, we walked hand in hand to Ryan's car. But when we got there, someone was already waiting for him: Elise Wilder.

I dropped his hand. "Seems like you already have other plans," I said. I turned on my heels and walked away, forcing myself not to look back. I could hear Ryan calling my name, then the low voice of the girl. I couldn't hear what she said to him, but it sounded urgent, almost hysterical.

I didn't miss the amber-colored glare she sent my way, either.

Ryan didn't follow me, which I guess said it all. Even Sam would have to see my side of things now.

I walked without thinking, my feet taking me in whatever direction they wanted. I finally emerged from my thoughts and noticed my surroundings. I was in the park, and it was past dark. I realized it was a stupid thing to do.

I glimpsed some movement out of the corner of my eye. I didn't slow down to take a picture, just lengthened my stride. I remembered the howling I had heard in the park and shivered at the thought.

I reassured myself that I'd taken a basic self-defense class but ignored the fact that one of the tips I had learned in it was to avoid isolated areas, especially when no one knew where you were.

I'd managed to outrun Nicholas once before when he was in his furrier form, but he was also a friendly werewolf. I had a feeling that whatever was following me wasn't as friendly.

CHAPTER SEVENTEEN

When I looked over my shoulder, I discovered a different kind of predator entirely.

"Daisy, please wait!" Duke. A perfect ending to a perfect day.

"Duke, you scared me," I said.

"I was driving by and saw you enter the park. I wanted to make sure you were safe," he said.

I was a little creeped out when I realized it had been him following me.

"It is not safe to walk here after dark alone. Let me give you a ride home."

In the distance, I heard a long, mournful howl and decided Duke was the lesser of two evils. And he, at least, was harmless. Whatever had made that noise probably was not.

I followed Duke to his car, which turned out to be a new Lexus. I wondered how a high school junior could afford a car like that. The fortune-telling business must be pretty profitable.

Then again, Nightshade High's parking lot was filled with everything from new Porsches to thirty-year-old Pintos.

He opened the passenger door for me, and a T-shirt fell from the seat. I picked it up, but he snatched it away, though not before I saw the college colors.

"Are you thinking of going there?" I asked.

"What?"

"To Cal State Fullerton," I said, motioning to the orange and navy shirt. I knew orange and navy were their colors because I'd been toying with the idea of going there myself.

Duke seemed perplexed for a moment. "Oh, yes, the T-shirt. I have been thinking of it. Do you know much about it?"

"Only by reputation," I admitted, "but it seems like a great school."

"What about you?" Duke said, relaxing and putting the car into drive. "Any idea of where you will be going?"

"Not yet," I confessed. "There are a few I like, but picking a college feels pretty overwhelming."

We made polite conversation on the way, but when he pulled into my driveway, things turned more serious.

Without asking permission, he took my right hand, flipped it palm up, and studied it intently.

He traced the longest line with a lone finger. I suppressed a tiny shiver—not of dread but of attraction.

"You have a strong life line, Daizee," he said.

"Er, thank you," I said. How had his arm ended up on the back of my seat?

"Daizee, have you thought any more about prom?"

"I've been busy." Lame excuse, but I didn't want to admit I'd been waiting for Ryan.

"And the boy you have been waiting for—he has not extended an invitation?" Maybe Duke *was* psychic. He'd certainly homed in on my thoughts quickly enough.

I shook my head. I didn't trust my voice enough to answer him.

"I wonder if this boy no longer returns your regard," he continued. "I have the utmost respect for you. I think we have much in common."

He leaned closer and captured a strand of my hair between his fingers. The smoothness of the gesture made me wonder how many other girls he'd practiced it on. Still, there was something intoxicating about his brilliant blue eyes. I stared into them.

"And we could have even more in common." His tone turned seductive as he moved closer still.

I was relieved when the porch light went on. For once, I was glad that Poppy was doing her usual spying. I was so not ready for anything Duke had in mind.

"I've got to go," I said. I got out of the car. "Thanks for the ride."

I hurried inside, kicking myself for being stupid enough to accept a ride home from Duke, even though my only alternative had been to roam around Nightshade with a killer on the loose. But I was also kicking myself for giving Ryan another chance. Obviously, whatever Elise needed was more important than a night alone with me.

CHAPTER EIGHTEEN

The next day, Ryan was in our last-period gym class, but he didn't look very well. He was grim faced and red eyed, and even had a bit of stubble. He almost looked like he'd been out drinking all night, but Ryan didn't drink. Or at least he didn't used to.

When the dismissal bell rang and I headed out to the parking lot, I heard his voice behind me. "Daisy, wait up. There's something I want to talk to you about."

I crossed my arms and sighed. He looked at me pleadingly. "I'm sorry about last night, but you don't understand the situation."

I just looked at him, then finally said, "Did it involve death or dismemberment?" Cold, I know, but I'm a girl with issues. Standing me up makes me cranky, especially since I had a dad who was a permanent no-show.

"No, but—"

"Then I don't want to hear it," I said.

I started to walk away, but he called after me, "I heard you got a ride home from Duke Sherrad."

"At least *he* cared enough to make sure I got home safely." The words were out of my mouth before I'd finished thinking them.

"What are you doing with that guy?" he said.

I stopped and whirled around, enraged. "I could ask you the same question about Elise!"

"Daisy, you've just got to trust me," Ryan said.

"You keep saying to trust you, but you won't tell me what's happening, you never show up when you say you will, and you're always with that girl."

"There's nothing going on between Elise and me," he said.

"Then what's with all the secrecy? If it's not Elise, then what is it?"

Ryan paused. "I can't tell you," he said.

"Then I can't do this anymore." I walked away, and he didn't stop me. I waited until I was out of sight before bursting into tears.

I couldn't believe it. The thing I'd been dreading had finally happened. Ryan had broken up with me. Hadn't he? Well, maybe technically I had broken up with him, but that was only because he didn't give me any other choice.

When I told my sisters, I was surprised at Rose's reaction.

"Give him a little space," Rose advised. "He'll come around."

"Space?" I said. "I've given him Grand Canyons of space."

"Maybe there's something going on that you don't know about," Rose continued.

I stared at her. "Like what? Besides that he's spending all his time with another girl? I *know* that."

"But you don't know why."

"Yes, I do," I said. "I know three reasons. Tall, brunette, and gorgeous."

I went upstairs a few minutes later. I wasn't getting much sympathy from my sister. I decided to hash things out with Samantha. I knocked on Poppy's bedroom door. "I'm going to take the car," I told her.

"Can you drop me off at Mort's?" Poppy said.

What? Usually she complained at least a little when I wanted to take the car, but she was actually smiling.

"Sure," I said, "but I may be a while. I'm going to Samantha's to hang out."

"Take your time. Gage is going to help me with my English lit homework. I've got to get my grade up to a C or Mom will kill me."

"Gage is going to help you?" I asked. Poppy didn't seem to find anything odd about the idea of a ghost helping her with her homework. And she was wearing her favorite top and perfume. And as gorgeous as Poppy normally is, she looked even prettier than usual. She looked like she was getting ready for a date instead of a night of studying.

"Sure. He's a senior, too. And he's positively brilliant. He helped me with physics last night."

"You mean he *was* a senior," I said as gently as I could. Poppy's growing attachment to Gage was making me nervous. I mean, talk about a relationship that wasn't going to go anywhere. Like I had room to talk—but at least my guy was alive.

"That's what I said," Poppy replied. She shrugged it off, but her smile had disappeared.

I dropped her off at Mort's and then worried about her the rest of the way to Sam's. Poppy talked tough, but in her heart, she was as soft as a marshmallow.

When I pulled up to the palatial Devereaux house, I was in for a shock. There was a large FOR SALE sign on the front lawn.

As I approached the front door, I could hear Samantha arguing with someone.

"You couldn't wait until I finished high school for this? It's already the end of my junior year."

I couldn't hear what the reply was, but the voice was a woman's. Mrs. Devereaux must be in town doing a little flyby parenting.

"And whose fault is that?" Sam said, her voice rising.

"Samantha, will you keep your voice down? We do not want to let every eavesdropping neighbor know our business." Sam's mother's voice was clearly identifiable now.

I felt like a creep listening in on their argument. I hastily rang the doorbell and waited.

Several minutes later, Mrs. Devereaux threw open the door. *What, no servants?* I thought.

I detected a hint of anger in her face before she carefully smoothed it away into an expression of bland pleasantness.

"Daisy Giordano," she said. She looked as enthused as I felt when hearing the news that there would be a pop quiz. In other words, not very. "What a lovely surprise."

In other words, polite people called first.

"Hello, Mrs. Devereaux. Is Samantha here?"

"Samantha is . . ." She paused, obviously trying to think up a way to get rid of me.

"Out of here," Samantha said from behind her. She brushed by her mother. "Let's go, Daisy!" she said as she walked out without a backward glance.

She headed for her car, but I stopped her. "I have my car. Why don't I drive?"

Sam didn't answer, but she got into the passenger seat. Her knuckles showed white as she clenched and unclenched her fists.

I drove silently for a few minutes, letting Samantha regain her composure.

"Do you want to talk about it?"

"No," Sam said.

She didn't say a word for the next half hour. We'd pretty much covered the whole town twice over, except the detours I'd made to avoid Ryan's house and the Wilder place. I felt a twinge at the thought of him but repressed it. Samantha's problems were bigger than mine.

Eventually, I pulled up in front of Slim's and turned off the motor. "How about a cup of coffee?"

Samantha finally smiled. "How about a chocolate shake instead?"

Things were bad if Sam was resorting to junk food.

When we entered the restaurant, the jukebox cut off in mid-song. The locals were used to it, but two stray tourists looked a little spooked when "Poison Cup" by M. Ward began to play. Probably just Lil's sad commentary on my love life.

Flo gave us a couple of menus and pointed to a booth in the back.

After we ordered a variety of high-calorie items, Samantha told me everything. Some things I'd suspected, like that her parents were having serious money troubles, but some things I didn't know, like that her dad was hardly ever home anymore and her mom had practically taken up permanent residence with Sam's grandparents in San Francisco.

"And they're getting a divorce," she said. "That's why they're selling the house. Mom wants me to move to San Francisco with her."

"Leave Nightshade? But you can't!" I was so shocked that

I barely noticed Flo putting our food on the table. The thought of losing Samantha scared me. She was a royal pain sometimes, but she was still my best friend.

"What else can I do?"

I pushed away my fries, suddenly no longer hungry. "What about your dad? Can't you live with him?"

"He's busy with his research. And when he's not doing that, he's busy with book tours."

"You should ask him, Samantha. Maybe he'll say yes. At least *try* to stay in Nightshade."

"Dad *did* get a three-bedroom condo in the hills by the university," she said. "Maybe I will ask him."

"Three bedrooms for one person? He probably got an extra room for you."

Sam started to say something, but she was distracted by someone coming in.

"What the hell?" she said. "What's Ryan doing with her?"

I didn't look up. I knew who I'd see standing next to Ryan. Elise Wilder.

"We broke up," I said. "That's what I came over to your house to talk about."

"You should have said something," she said.

"You have bigger things to worry about than my pathetic love life."

"That creep," she said. "I can't believe he broke up with you this close to prom."

"Would it have been any better to wait until *after* prom?" I didn't think so.

Sam shrugged. "Maybe not," she admitted. She paused, "You're going with Duke now, of course."

"What? No, of course not. I'm skipping prom," I said.

"You can't!" she said. "Promise me you'll at least think about—I don't believe it. They're coming over here."

"You've got to be kidding me," I said. But she wasn't. Ryan and Elise were almost at our table.

Could my day get any better?

"Hi, Daisy," Ryan said solemnly.

Samantha and I exchanged glances. Was Ryan clueless, or was he trying to rub my face in it?

"Ryan, Elise," I said, as civilly as I could—which, truthfully, wasn't very civilly at all.

"Elise thought it would be a good idea if we talked—to clear up any misunderstandings."

The jukebox kicked on. "Should I Stay or Should I Go?" by the Clash. I knew the answer.

"Sorry, Ryan, we were just leaving," I said. I stood and grabbed the check. "Maybe some other time." Yeah, I'd be hanging out with my ex and his new girlfriend. Not in this lifetime.

CHAPTER NINETEEN

For the rest of the week I was in a terrible mood. Once, when Elise Wilder and I happened to brush against each other in the hall between classes, she gave me a little shove. I couldn't help but give her a little shove back, causing her to drop her books.

She stooped to the floor to retrieve them and looked up at me, her amber eyes fierce. "Thanks a lot," she hissed.

"Oh no, Elise, thank *you*," I said sarcastically. I didn't know I had it in me to be that bitchy.

"What were you doing at my cousin's house?" she demanded.

"Wh—what do you mean?"

"I know it was you," she said, her strange eyes gleaming. "The place had your stench all over it."

"I don't know what you mean," I said. Like I was going to tell Ryan's new girlfriend anything, even if she was related to Mr. Davis.

"I'm going to ask you again. Why were you there?" She

slammed me up against the wall. I read the threat in her eyes. The girl was seriously strong.

"Do you lift weights?" I asked.

"Don't screw with me, Giordano," she snarled. "So far, I've just been toying with you." To my surprise, I thought I saw tears in her eyes, but she brushed them away angrily.

We were starting to attract some attention. Bane Paxton glanced over and started heading our way.

"Look," I said. "I was trying to help find out who killed Mr. Davis, that's all."

The tension left her body, but she didn't release her hold on me. "If I ever find out who did it—"

Bane touched her arm. "Let her go, Elise," he said. "People are starting to notice your chat with Daisy here. It would not be good if this got back to your grandmother."

Elise nodded tersely and released me. Bane took her arm to lead her away, but Elise whipped around and whispered fiercely, "If you find out anything, anything at all . . ."

I nodded, not trusting myself to speak. I looked across the crowd and saw Duke staring at me. He walked over to me a minute later.

"Are you okay?" he said. He put his arm around me. When I saw the concern in his eyes, I resisted the impulse to shrug it off.

"I'm fine," I said. "It was just a misunderstanding."

"He's a fool, you know," Duke said. "To choose someone like Elise Wilder over you." He said her name contemptuously.

"Do you know her?" I asked.

"Only by reputation," he replied. "She will come to a bad end, mark my words."

"Is that a prediction?"

He met my eyes, and it was like looking into the surface of a frozen lake. "That's an observation. I wouldn't be surprised if she had something to do with her cousin's death."

The bell rang, and as I headed to class, I wondered about Duke's words. I didn't like Elise Wilder much either, but Duke had sounded like he absolutely loathed the sight of her. What was that all about?

My mood changed at the end of the day when Samantha approached me at my locker, smiling ear to ear. "Daisy, you're a genius!" she exclaimed, and gave me a hug.

"I've always known it, but sadly, no one else seems to be aware of the fact. Is there anything in particular that I'm genius about?"

"I did it!" Sam explained. "I asked my dad if I could live with him and stay in Nightshade until I graduate, and he said yes. And I owe it all to you. I never would have asked him without you convincing me to do it."

"That's great news, Sam." I smiled at her.

"Can you do me a favor and not say anything to anybody? At least not for a while. I need to think about what I'm going to tell everybody."

"Tell them the truth, Sam," I said. "Nobody cares about what kind of house you live in. They care about you."

"They care about the Divine Devereaux," she said. "Not about me."

"I care," I said.

"You and Sean are the only two people who know the real me," she said.

I protested. "And Rachel and Jordan and . . ."

She cut me off. "Enough about me."

"Samantha, you have more friends than any girl I know. Certainly more than I do."

"You have lots of friends, Daisy," she said. "You just don't know it."

I blushed. This from the girl who was convinced that most of Nightshade High only liked her for her money or her popularity.

"Well, this is cause for celebration," I said. "Let's go to Slim's and get shakes."

"Okay!" said Samantha enthusiastically. It would be nice to celebrate something after a gloomy couple of weeks in Nightshade.

At Slim's we spotted Poppy at the register with a couple of to-go containers. After she paid, I waved her over to our table.

"I thought you were at Mort's," I said.

She held up two gigantic sodas. "Caffeine break," she said.

"Two sodas?"

"One is for Gage," she said. "Even though he can't really drink it, he has one to keep me company." She realized she'd slipped and glanced at Sam in alarm.

Samantha slid over in the booth. "Have a seat," she said. Poppy sat next to her.

"Poppy's dating a ghost," I explained. "He haunts Mort's."

Samantha just shrugged. "You Giordano girls," she said. "You really know how to pick 'em."

"His name is Gage. He's a perfectly nice guy," she pointed out.

"I'm sure he is," said Sam.

"I know you and Rose aren't thrilled about me and Gage because he's a ghost," Poppy said to me.

"We just want you to be happy, but I don't see how things with Gage could . . ."

"Work out," she finished my sentence. "I know. But it's just not fair. I finally meet a guy I could really lo—like and he's already dead."

Samantha put her arm around Poppy as my sister brushed away a tear. "He went to San Carlos High, you know. We could have met. We could have been happy."

I had the impulse to tell Poppy to go for it, to be with the guy she loved, no matter what. But then I remembered I wasn't exactly in any position to be dispensing advice on romance.

Duke walked into Slim's, and I had to repress a groan. When he saw us, he flashed a bright smile and hurried over.

Sam kicked me under the table and said, so that only I could hear, "Bird in the hand, Giordano."

To Duke she said, "What a nice surprise. Won't you join us?"

"Thank you so much, Samantha," he said politely. "I would love to."

"There's not much room," I said. I wasn't in the mood for Duke's big blue eyes and flirtatious smile.

"Make some room," Sam commanded. "Slide over." I did it reluctantly, but Sam had on her *I'll hurt you if you don't* face.

There was a moment of silence, then Duke said, "Daisy, I would be honored if you would allow me to do a tarot reading sometime. Perhaps Saturday night?"

"I'm kind of busy," I said.

I looked away and saw Penny glaring at me from her seat, which was in the prime stalking-Duke section. That could have been what motivated my next words.

"What about right now?"

"Now?" Duke seemed oddly taken aback. "I—my tarot cards are in my car."

"Go get them. I'll get us something to drink." Samantha jumped up and went over to the counter, where Flo was reading a magazine. After a brief conversation, Sam returned carrying a pitcher of soda.

"Refreshments," she said, brandishing the pitcher in the air.

Duke came back with a pack of tarot cards. He gestured to the cards. "Samantha, would you like for me to do a reading for you as well?"

"I'll pass this time," she replied.

I felt self-conscious as I cut the cards. Duke's blue eyes watched my every move while I shuffled the deck with shaky hands. I handed it back to him and he laid out the cards.

He was silent for a moment. He frowned. He stared at the cards in front of him for several long minutes. It was like he had been reading *Inscrutability for Beginners.*

"I see a man," he said hesitantly.

A man? Tall, dark, and handsome perhaps? Had he been giving everybody the same line?

"He is still alive," Duke continued. "He's waiting for you. He wants to come home."

Poppy stilled. "Who is waiting?" she asked, her breathing light and erratic.

"Which card represents a man?" Samantha asked.

Duke seemed flustered. His hands swept in a wide arc and knocked over the pitcher, which was still half full of soda, spilling it all over the cards. They turned into a sodden mess, but I was already out of my seat.

Nausea churned in my stomach as I made my way to the exit. If Duke's reading was a joke, it wasn't a very funny one.

Tears blurred my vision. I had to get out of there.

I brushed by a tall figure as I left. The jukebox burst into "Hungry Like the Wolf" by Duran Duran.

"Daisy?" It was Ryan, but I didn't bother to stop. I was running away from my past, even though it seemed determined to catch up with me.

Poppy came after me, of course. "What was that all about?"

"I have no idea," I said, "but I don't trust Duke for a minute."

Samantha followed us outside a minute later. "I paid the check," she said. "I figured you wouldn't want to go back inside now that Ryan's there."

"I know. I don't feel like facing anyone right now, especially not him. I'm just going home." I looked up at the sky. Since we'd been inside, the weather had grown gray and chilly. It matched my mood perfectly.

"Hey, wait a second," Samantha said. "I have a better idea. How about a little retail therapy?"

"Yeah, Daisy, that will cheer you up," Poppy said. "Let's go to the mall."

"What about Gage?" I sniffed.

"He'll understand," she said.

"I still need to get a prom dress," Sam said as we got into her car.

"Not me," I said sadly.

"You should go buy a dress and go to prom," she said firmly. "With or without Ryan Mendez."

After I thought about it for a few minutes, I realized Samantha was right. Besides, I had put a lot of energy into helping set up the prom. I shouldn't miss it just because of a breakup. I nodded decisively.

"I'm going to call Mom to let her know we're going shopping and make sure it's okay if we use the plastic," Poppy said. Mom had given each of us a credit card for emergencies.

Mom seemed thrilled to hear that her two youngest daughters were going shopping instead of moping around the house. I guess she figured nothing weird could happen at a mall.

As we stood in front of the store directory and tried to figure out where to start our shopping spree, Poppy suddenly seemed doubtful about our mall mission.

"You know, I don't have a date, either," Poppy said.

"Why don't you ask Gage?" Samantha suggested.

Poppy and I stared at her.

"What? Isn't that his name?"

"I can't take a ghost to the prom," Poppy protested, but I could tell she liked the idea. "Can I?"

"Why not?" I said. "It's Nightshade. People probably won't even notice." And I didn't care if they did, as long as my sister smiled again.

"You're right," Poppy said slowly. "Why not?" She grinned. "I'll ask him tonight. Let's go try on dresses!"

Both Samantha and Poppy were marathon shoppers. Finally, after about three hours of fruitless searching, I was ready for a break.

"I see a Coffee Bean and Tea Leaf over there," I said, pointing in the direction of the food court, "and I'm not trying on one more dress until I get a blended coffee."

"Does she exist on coffee and chocolate?" Samantha said to Poppy.

"Pretty much," she replied.

"That's not true," I protested. "I cook all the time."

"She *is* a good cook," Poppy admitted.

"Yes, but all that coffee will stunt her growth."

"Now you tell me," I said in mock dismay. "Now that it's too late for my gymnastics career." There was a time when gymnastics was my life, but then an early growth spurt ended my sport of choice before it even began.

Samantha must have detected a little sadness in my voice, because she linked arms with me. "C'mon, let's get you that coffee."

Refreshed by the caffeine, I was ready to tackle the search again. Samantha and Poppy both found their dresses, but everything I tried on was either too tight, too short, or too revealing.

An hour later, I spotted it. It was strapless, pale gold with a beaded bodice and skirt, and much more sophisticated than anything I'd tried on before.

I held it up in front of me. "What do you guys think?" I wasn't sure the pale gold would work with my coloring.

"It's perfect," Samantha said. "Go try it on."

When I stepped out of the dressing room, I could tell by their expressions that I'd found my dress.

Then I looked at the price tag and gasped. "Poppy, Mom's going to have a coronary," I said, showing her the amount.

Poppy looked at the price and shrugged. "That's only a little more than my dress cost," she said. "But if it makes you feel any better, it's on sale. Ten percent off."

I did the calculations in my head. "Okay, I'll buy it."

I went back to change into my regular clothes but found myself reluctant to take the dress off. It would have been perfect to wear to the prom with Ryan.

"His loss," I muttered under my breath. After I dressed and handed over my emergency credit card, I was ready to head home, but Poppy and Samantha had other ideas.

"Now shoes!" they exclaimed. I bit back a groan, but I had to admit that shopping with them was more fun than I expected.

By the time the mall closed, I had a dress, I had shoes, and I was almost convinced I didn't need a guy. Any guy but Ryan, that is.

CHAPTER TWENTY

After the shopping spree, I was glad to get back home, where I could relax. I rushed to our warm, familiar kitchen and got out a pot. I would make mac and cheese from scratch with three kinds of cheese for dinner. It was a perfect night for comfort food, and this had been my dad's favorite meal.

After I put the food in the oven, Poppy said, very casually, "What do you think about what Duke said?"

"I don't know what to think. Part of me hopes it's true, that Dad is out there somewhere, just trying to get home," I admitted.

Poppy's eyes filled with tears. "Do you think it's really possible?"

"I don't know that either, but I'm going to find out whether Duke's a phony. And I'm going to start with Penny."

"Why Penny?"

"She's the biggest gossip in school," I replied. "And besides, she's been hanging all over him. It would have been easy for Duke to pump her for information since he's staying at her house."

"True," she said. "It's not like she'd need any encouragement."

I was a little embarrassed about seeing everyone at school after I had made such a scene at Slim's. And I was going to shove Penny's pom-poms down her throat if she said a word about it. But it was mostly business as usual at Nightshade High, at least until I ran into Duke in the hallway.

"Daizee, I was worried about you. You rushed out in the middle of our reading."

"I was . . . upset."

Duke said, "I do not control what I see. I am only the conduit."

He appeared contrite, but I wasn't buying it.

"Just forget it, Duke," I said through gritted teeth.

"But Daisy, I admire you so much. You are so strong. You even killed vampire scum." He said the last words like he smelled something bad.

"How did you find out about that?"

"I have my ways." He smiled mysteriously.

"My friends were in danger," I said, thinking back to that scary time last fall when the cheerleaders were being taken out by a vamp one by one. "It's not like I just hate vampires."

His face darkened as he leaned closer. "If I had my way, they'd all . . ."

He didn't finish his sentence. He didn't really need to. That was a side of Duke I'd never seen before, and it seriously gave me the creeps.

I caught up with Penny in the lunch line and confronted her.

"What exactly did you tell Duke about me?"

"We have better things to do than talk about *you*, Giordano," she sniffed. "Get over yourself already."

"Answer the question, Penny. Did he ask about my family? My . . . father?"

"I told you he didn't ask me anything about you or your family the whole time he's been in Nightshade," she insisted.

I wasn't sure why, but I had a feeling that Penny was telling the truth. Call it my detective instinct. The girl was a gossip but not an outright liar. Plenty of other people knew about my family scandal, but I couldn't believe they would blab it to Duke. And how did he find out about the vampire? Besides my family, Samantha, Ryan, and Chief Mendez, the only people in town who knew about that were the members of the Nightshade City Council. There's no way Duke could know about that. Unless he really was psychic.

Penny interrupted my thoughts. "Have you heard his latest prediction?"

"What now? Did he predict you'll be prom queen?"

"No," she said, looking offended that I obviously found such a thing impossible. "It's Poppy. He predicted pain, loss, and death all around her. She didn't tell you?"

"No," I said. This prediction thing was getting serious. My stomach clenched at the thought of my sister in danger. "Thanks for telling me."

I was worried for the rest of the day. Even though Penny was not the most trustworthy person I knew, she'd sounded sincere. She really believed Poppy was in danger.

After school, Poppy went to Mort's to visit Gage as usual. At home, I paced anxiously, waiting for her safe return. Midnight followed me, rubbing up against my legs. When the doorbell rang, I practically ran to answer it. I was shocked to see Ryan standing on the porch.

"Hey," he said sheepishly. "I heard the rumors going around school about what Duke said about Poppy. I figured you'd be worried, and I wanted to see how you're doing."

I couldn't help but smile a little bit. Ryan may have been my ex, but he still knew me better than anyone else.

"Come in," I said. "I mean, if you want to."

Ryan followed me to the living room, where we sat down on the couch with Midnight snuggled between us, purring loudly.

"Did Duke say something that upset you at Slim's the other day?" he asked. "I saw you crying in the parking lot."

I nodded, embarrassed that Ryan had witnessed my total breakdown.

"Why do you listen to that guy, anyway?" Ryan asked. "He's a jerk, Daisy. Do you really think he's a true seer?"

"I don't know," I said. "Some of his predictions are coming

true." I didn't mention that I actually hoped the one about my father was true. "But this last one . . . What if Poppy is in danger? Nothing can happen to her. I can't lose someone else I love. I just can't." I couldn't stop shaking.

Ryan pulled me into his arms. "Shh," he whispered as he stroked my hair, "it's going to be all right." But it wasn't. It was almost unbearable being held by him after so much time apart.

"There's something I need to tell you," he said softly.

Being this close to him, looking into his green eyes, I knew for sure that he loved me. Suddenly, the events of the past few weeks made sense.

"You're a werewolf," I said in a hushed voice. How could I have missed it?

"How did you know?" he said.

"I figured it out," I said. "Why didn't you tell me? How long have you known?"

"A while," he admitted. "But I was scared to tell you. I knew you didn't like Nicholas dating Rose."

"Because he broke her heart last time," I said, "not because he's a werewolf."

"I know that now," he admitted. He took my hand. "I'm sorry I didn't tell you sooner."

"Who else knows?" I asked.

"My dad knows. The rest of the council, too."

I stared at him. Sometimes he seemed like a stranger. There was obviously a lot I didn't know about Ryan. "It was you. You were the Were fighting with Nicholas. Rose knew, didn't she?"

"Yes, it was me," Ryan admitted. "When I first turned, I wanted to fight with everyone, especially other Weres. Nicholas has had more time to gain control. He didn't want to fight. I didn't mean to hurt him."

"I can't believe that Rose didn't tell me."

"She wanted to, but I made her promise to let me be the one to tell you. But I kept putting it off, and things kept getting worse and worse between us. And then Duke was always sniffing around. I'm telling you, Daisy, he's bad news."

"I don't want to talk about Duke," I said. "What's the deal with Elise?"

"She was helping me through it," he said. "Strictly shifter to shifter," he added after a quick look at my face. "At first she actually thought I might have something to do with her cousin's death. She confronted me at my first city council meeting."

I remembered her strength when she pushed me up against the wall that day in school. I feared getting on the bad side of Elise Wilder.

"Why would she think that?" I wondered.

"I was near the scene of the crime," he said. "I was at the park the night it happened."

What was Ryan doing at the park that night? Mr. Davis had been attacked the night Ryan first stood me up. Aloud, I said, "What made her change her mind?"

"Well, you heard what Nicholas said. There was no scent of a werewolf on the body. Those marks were made by a human trying to make it look like a werewolf attack. But despite the facts, at first Elise was suspicious of me, and of every new werewolf in town. Then she realized that instead of alienating city council members, we could all be working together to find the real killer. So she finally stopped blaming everyone else and started trusting us."

I felt a little ashamed to think that I hadn't totally trusted Chief Mendez and Nicholas. How could I think they would ever cover up for a murderer? I also felt ashamed that I hadn't trusted Ryan. Maybe I could learn a thing or two from Elise.

"She's been a good friend to me, Daisy," Ryan continued. "She's had her shifting power a lot longer than I have. When . . . the change started happening to me, I told her how I was terrified that being a Were would mean losing you. So she helped me learn to control a shift. I'm getting pretty good at it now."

I had to admit, I was touched. "So when you two wanted to talk to me that day in the diner . . ."

"I told Elise you had broken up with me, and she wanted to try to talk you into giving me another chance," Ryan said. "I knew I'd have a hard time doing it on my own. But Elise thought that if she was able to tell you how she and her boyfriend deal with the shifting, you might feel better about things."

"Her boyfriend?"

"Bane Paxton," he said. "They've only been together for a few weeks."

"But I thought . . ."

"I know what you thought," he said. "But I only have eyes for you."

I sat in silence, trying to process the information.

Ryan cleared his throat and said, "So I hear you're going to prom with Duke Sherrad." He looked down at his hands.

"Who told you that?"

"Are you?"

"He asked me," I admitted, "but I haven't said yes."

"You haven't?" Ryan perked up. "Daisy, that's great news!"

I gave him a level stare. "I might, though, since no one else has asked me."

"I'm asking you," Ryan said. "Daisy Giordano, may I have the pleasure of your company at the Nightshade High prom?"

"I'd love to go with you," I replied. "But I'm still mad at you. You should have told me about being a werewolf."

He hesitated. "You're right."

"No more secrets," I said. "And no more disappearing or leaving me hanging. If you need to be alone, just say so."

Ryan sobered. "Daisy, everyone has secrets. But I promise you I'll never stand you up again. I'll never hurt you again."

CHAPTER TWENTY-ONE

The day of prom finally arrived. We still hadn't figured out who killed Mr. Davis, but Mom and Chief Mendez were working on it, so I decided to give my detective side a night off and go all out for prom.

It was a full day of preparations. My first stop was the park, where I supervised the volunteers who were setting up the Dark Carnival after party. Then Sam, Poppy, and I went to get our hair and nails done at a salon. Afterward, we stopped for a box of donuts at the new place across from Slim's.

"Conveniently located," Poppy said with a snicker, meaning the donut shop's close proximity to the police department.

We went home with the donuts, and I made iced lattes. We'd be up late so we needed the caffeine. Then I tried not to break a nail or move my head at all and risk disturbing my coiffure.

I couldn't wait to put on my dress. I couldn't wait for the night to start.

"What are we going to do for the next"—I checked my watch—"four hours?"

Surprisingly, the time passed quickly, once the rest of the girls arrived. And it took longer than I thought to put on my makeup and dress.

I'd just rechecked my hair when the doorbell rang and the guys started to arrive.

"How's Gage getting here?" I asked Poppy.

"Nicholas is bringing him," she said. She lowered her voice. "In one of the hearses. We're hoping he can get into the limo without any problems."

Poppy looked amazing in a long red silk dress, her hair done in a style that made her look like a 1940s movie star.

Chief Mendez came by and dropped Ryan off. The limo was going to pick everyone up at my house and drop everyone off at home after the prom. The chief pulled the limo driver aside and had a brief talk with him. I'm sure it involved promises of pain and suffering if any alcohol crossed our lips.

I hadn't really thought about drinking, anyway. I already felt like champagne bubbles were sparkling through my veins whenever I looked at Ryan.

He had on a black tux, white shirt, and a champagne-colored vest and tie. It took my breath away, but I managed to pin his boutonniere on the lapel of his jacket successfully, although with shaking hands.

He handed me a corsage of freesias and white daisies and whispered, "I told the florist that daisies are my favorite." It was corny, but it made me smile.

Rose and Nicholas arrived with Gage in tow. I don't know how he did it, but Gage looked very handsome, almost flesh and blood in a severe black tuxedo. He brought Poppy a white gardenia wrist corsage.

"You look so real," I said, reaching out to touch him, but he jumped back.

"I have to save my energy," he said. "I don't know how long I can sustain this. And I really want to dance with Poppy."

"Of course you do," I said. "Sorry, I just didn't think."

Samantha cleared her throat, and Sean looked around, confused. The light dawned, and he handed her an arrangement of red roses that went well with her beautiful white dress with black lace.

A bunch of parents showed up to take photos. I was relieved to see that Ryan and his dad were getting along again. Both Rose and Nicholas helped Mom take photos. Lots and lots of photos. I wondered if Gage would show up in any of them.

Samantha's dad even showed up. I hadn't seen him in a long time, not since the good old days when our families used to be close. He was tall and attractive, with salt-and-pepper hair that made him look a little bit like George Clooney—or at least that's what I heard Sean's mom say when she didn't think we were listening. He didn't talk much, but he smiled whenever he caught sight of Samantha.

We had reservations at Chanticlair's, a posh restaurant in San Carlos. Nightshade didn't have much to offer in the way of fine dining, unless you counted Slim's.

We all piled into the limousine. Sam and Sean, Jordan and Wyatt, Rachel and Adam, Poppy and Gage, Candy and her date—Jared something, a senior from some private school— and Ryan and me.

Chanticlair's was packed with kids from Nightshade High as well as San Carlos High. It must be prom night for our rival school as well. I spotted Chelsea and Cassandra Morris and waved. They were seated at a table with two cute guys I didn't know.

Chelsea wore a beautiful deep green gown, while Cassandra wore a short hot pink number that should have clashed with her red hair but instead looked wonderful. Chelsea and Cassandra were seniors at San Carlos, and Chelsea cheered for the Squids. Awful name, I know, but since the Nightshade mascot was the Sea Monster, we didn't have a lot of room to talk.

I went over to say hi to them and to thank them for the loan of the yearbook.

I noticed Chelsea was staring at Gage. "Isn't that . . . ?" she trailed off.

"Gage Atwood," I confirmed. "It's complicated."

"But he's dead," Chelsea burst out.

"Shh, Poppy's really sensitive about it," I said.

"But how—?"

"You should know, anything's possible in Nightshade."

Elise Wilder entered the restaurant on the arm of Bane Paxton. He paled when he saw Chelsea but then recovered quickly. They'd been involved, briefly, a few months ago, but Chelsea was a completely different person now.

Elise looked beautiful, of course. Her hair was loose and was in a wild riot of curls. She wore a black dress with a lace bustier thing that both revealed and concealed her cleavage. The dress suited her well. It looked as dangerous as she did.

We were seated by a very intimidating man in an expensive suit. I glanced over at Poppy and Gage. They looked perfect together, but I wondered if he felt uncomfortable away from Mort's, at a restaurant. I mean, could ghosts eat? I didn't think so. What would he do when it was time to order?

Gage did the sweetest thing. He ordered something he knew Poppy loved and fed her bites of it from his plate.

Back in the limo, Samantha announced, "We need to frisk the guys for booze before we get there. We'll lose the deposit if anyone gets caught drinking."

I didn't have to worry about Ryan. He didn't drink. But frisking him didn't sound unappealing. I mean, we wouldn't want the prom committee to lose their deposit.

"I'm under orders to frisk you later," I teased Ryan.

"I can't wait," he replied. His tone made me blush.

The limo slowly made its way up the driveway to the Wilder mansion, which was lined by hundred-year-old oak trees. I held my breath. It was like something out of a movie.

Bianca, the woman I had met on our last visit, was on hostess duty. She showed us to the ballroom.

"Have a good time, Daisy, Ryan," she said. It was spooky how she knew our names.

Prom was being held in the grand ballroom, which had a black-and-white marble floor and was decorated in twinkly white lights, balloons, and flowers by the pound. Jordan Kelley was on the prom committee and had convinced her dad to donate the flowers. He owned a chain of florist shops as well as the only plant nursery in town. The room looked like Mr. Kelley had donated half his stock to the cause.

We found our table, which was set with crisp linens and gleaming gold tableware. With their Were blood, it's no wonder the Wilders weren't too fond of silver. There were towering centerpieces of white roses, lilies, and orchids, tied together with gold ribbon.

Gage murmured to Poppy. "There were white roses at my funeral. White roses. My mother pricked her finger on a thorn." His voice was choked, and his form seemed to go in and out of focus.

"Gage, are you okay?" Poppy asked. And his figure solidified, but he seemed shaken.

He smiled at her reassuringly. "Don't think you're going to get out of that dance. I'm going to dance with you if it's the last thing I ever do."

Penny made a grand entrance on the arm of Duke Sherrad. Everyone stopped talking and stared, but possibly not for the reason Penny had hoped. She preened at the attention, but all the fuss was caused by her highlighter-yellow evening gown, which was patterned with blue peacock feathers. The bodice of her gown was made of something resembling blue glitter, and she wore matching peacock feathers in her hair, which gave her an unfortunate resemblance to Big Bird.

Her escort was slightly more sedate in a black dinner jacket, although his yellow tie and vest made him look like an angry bumblebee.

Ryan growled when he saw Duke, but I gave his arm a little squeeze. "Just ignore him," I said.

But that proved to be easier said than done. Duke and Penny strutted to our table. She ignored me, though, and rushed to Samantha's side. "You look absolutely stunning in that dress," Penny said, then paused, obviously waiting for a return compliment. She waited a long time, since Sam only smiled and said, "Thank you."

Poppy rolled her eyes when Penny clamped her hand on Duke's arm and dragged him forward. "Doesn't Duke look handsome, Poppy?"

Poppy didn't take her eyes from Gage. "Yeah, sure," she said.

Duke made little effort to conceal his annoyance with Penny. He took her hand off his arm and made a bow in front of me. "Would you like to dance, Daizee?"

"No, thanks," I said, and turned back to my date.

I thought Ryan would come unglued, but he bared his teeth in the semblance of a smile. "Sorry, Duke, looks like her dance card is full tonight."

From the look on Penny's face, I thought she was going to lay into me, but to my surprise, she let Duke have it instead.

"I am your date, Duke, not Daisy."

"I only asked you because I was sick of hearing you whine about how you didn't have a date," he replied. Was it just my imagination or had his accent faded?

The rest of the table looked away, but I stared at Duke's face. His petulant expression reminded me of someone else, someone I'd seen recently.

"Oh, yeah?" countered Penny. "Well, I'm sick of hearing your phony predictions!"

Now *that* I didn't expect. Penny had been Duke's loudest advocate.

Duke looked flustered. "How dare you call me a phony!"

Penny rolled her eyes. "Please. A real fortune-teller wouldn't need a book called *A Goof-Ball's Guide to Fortune-Telling*, now would he? I saw it in your room, Duke."

Duke turned a deep shade of scarlet and looked enraged. "Of all the families in Nightshade, I get stuck staying with the one with the nosiest, most meddlesome teenage daughter!" he snapped.

I also didn't expect it when Penny doubled up her fist and punched Duke in the stomach.

What Penny didn't expect was the round of applause.

CHAPTER TWENTY-TWO

After Duke and Penny stomped off to continue their fight in private, the mood at our table lightened considerably.

About ten minutes later, I noticed that Penny was alone in a corner. I scanned the room, but there was no sign of Duke.

"I'll be right back," I said to Ryan.

The worst that could happen was that Penny would laugh in my face. "Would you like to join us at our table?" I asked.

From the expression on her face, I expected her to say something snotty, but instead she offered a small smile. "If you're sure?"

"Of course!" I said. "Besides, I want to find out where you got that right hook of yours."

Penny giggled with me. "Thanks, Daisy," she said. Back at the table, she immediately started ignoring me again, but I was fine with that. Penny and I would never be best friends, but I'd gained new respect for her.

A slow song started, and Ryan grabbed my hand and led me to the center of the dance floor. As I nuzzled closer to him, I thought that the way he smelled was way better than my two favorite scents in the world.

"You smell better than chocolate," I said to him.

"You do, too," he said. He put his lips to the soft skin of my neck, and I shivered. "You taste better, too."

Our lips met in a long, sweet kiss. A little while later, I emerged from my Ryan-induced fog and looked over at Poppy.

She and Gage danced cheek to cheek. Her eyes were shut, and she was so close to him that it was hard to tell where he stopped and she began.

It had been a minor miracle, an act of incredible will on Gage's part, that had allowed him to take corporeal form. I wondered what the consequences would be, besides the obvious, which was that eventually, Poppy and Gage would have to go their separate ways. But they were clearly falling in love, and the world couldn't be so cruel as to tear them apart now.

The disco ball put sparkles in their hair as they revolved slowly under its glow.

"Does Gage look a bit . . . shaky to you?" I asked Ryan.

Ryan glanced over quickly. "Maybe." He pulled me a fraction closer to him. "But I'm not interested in Gage right now." He nibbled on my ear.

I was having a hard time concentrating, but I persisted. "No, really. Look."

Gage was almost transparent, going in and out of focus, but nobody else seemed to notice.

Ryan waltzed me over to where they were dancing.

"Gage, you're fading." I said in a quiet voice.

Poppy didn't lift her head from his shoulder. "Quit joking."

"I'm serious," I said.

Poppy stared into Gage's eyes for a long moment. "He's just going back to being incorporeal," she finally said.

"No, it's different. We don't have much time," Gage said. "It's for good this time."

"No," she said, loudly. A few heads turned, but when she pretended to smile brightly, they went back to whatever they were doing.

The sheen of tears in Gage's eyes convinced her. "I love you, Poppy," he said.

Ryan and I looked away to give them some privacy, but I heard her say, "I love . . ."

When I looked over, my sister was alone on the dance floor, surrounded by pain, loss, and death. Fake psychic or not, Duke had been right.

I grabbed her hand and led her off the dance floor as tears gushed from her eyes. She kept her head down, so that no one could see.

"I'm going to call Rose to pick me up," she said.

"I'll go with you," I said. "Just let me tell Ryan."

"No, Daisy," Poppy said. "You stay. It's your prom, too. And Gage and I had a great prom before he . . . had to go."

I watched her leave, and then Ryan took my hand. "She'll be okay," he said gently.

"I know," I said. "But it's just not fair. She finally finds someone . . ."

"It makes you think, doesn't it?" Ryan said. "About making the most of the time we have together."

He sounded as if he knew something I didn't. "Ryan?" I said, but he didn't answer. He just drew me close and held me tight.

After a few more dances, I headed for the restroom to freshen my makeup and to make sure that I hadn't sweated through my gorgeous dress.

That's when I saw Duke head for the stairs. He was going into the part of the mansion that was off-limits to prom guests. There was something furtive about the way he slunk away. I decided to follow him.

CHAPTER TWENTY-THREE

My high heels would make too much noise on the marble staircase, so I kicked them off and tucked them in a corner before I went after Duke.

He seemed to be searching for something in particular. We were on the top floor of the mansion, which was clearly private living space for the Wilder family.

He almost caught me when he glanced back unexpectedly, but I ducked behind a huge statue. When I got the nerve up to peek out from my hiding spot, Duke had disappeared.

I tiptoed to where he'd been standing. The door was open a crack, so I looked inside. Duke was standing in what was obviously a lavishly decorated woman's bedroom. I suspected it was Mrs. Wilder's.

There was a cup of tea cooling on a carved ebony tray. Duke crossed to it and fumbled in his pocket. He found whatever he was looking for and dropped it into the tea.

I entered the room. "Is that how you did it?"

"Daizee," he said. "What are you doing here?"

"I could ask you the same question, but I already know the answer."

"Don't keep me in suspense," Duke said. He smiled nastily. I don't know why I ever thought he was cute.

"You poisoned Mr. Davis. And you used his own garden to do it."

"Why would I want to kill Mr. Davis?"

"Maybe because he knew that you're not actually a high school student and he threatened to expose you?" I ventured.

"You have no proof," he said, but he didn't look so cocky. I noticed that his accent had completely disappeared.

"Are you sure? I saw a photo at his house of three guys in a college play. I thought I recognized one of them. It took me a while to put it together because back then you had blond hair and glasses."

"Very good, Daisy," he said. "It's a pity you have such liberal views of those paranormal scum. We could have used someone with your brains." He drew a gun from his jacket.

I'd made a huge mistake confronting Duke, I realized as I stared down the barrel of a gun. I needed to stall him.

"What was the deal with the T-shirt in your car?" I asked, but I already knew the answer. The shirt I'd seen hadn't been for Cal State at all. Why would Duke want to go there? He'd already graduated from college with Mr. Davis.

"You're observant, Daisy," he said. "Yes, the T-shirt in my car was from my alma mater, Charles Fey College. A careless mistake on my part. I'd been assigned to track Dexter even back then."

Now I knew the real reason he had killed Mr. Davis. "You're part of the Scourge!"

"I'm impressed you figured that out," he said. "Now drink," he ordered, shoving the teacup to my lips.

Suddenly, the door opened and Bianca stood in front of us. She moved in a blur, and a second later she was gone and Midnight stood in her place. She flew at Duke and raked her claws in his face. He screamed and dropped the gun.

I dropped the tea as I scrambled to pick up the gun. I held it, hands shaking, as Duke grabbed my cat.

"Let her go," I said. "Or I swear I'll shoot."

He released his grip, and with an angry hiss Midnight came to my side and nudged my leg affectionately.

A minute later, Bianca stood beside me again. "Give me the gun."

"Don't do it, Daisy," Duke begged. "Come with me and I'll bring you to your father!"

My resolve wavered for a moment. Could it be that the Scourge had my father and that Duke really could take me to where he was? I thought how wonderful it would be to see him again, to hug him, just to know he was still alive.

"Daisy!" said Bianca urgently. She had saved my life. Duke had done nothing but lie to me and everyone in Nightshade. I handed her the gun.

"Good. You're doing great. There's a phone on the bedside table," Bianca said. "Call the police. Ask for Chief Mendez. Do not speak to anybody else."

After I called the chief and explained the situation, I helped Bianca tie up Duke while we waited for help to arrive.

"It was lucky you found us," I said.

She hesitated. "Not exactly," she confessed. "The council was suspicious of Duke from the beginning. Duke's not his real name. It's Herbert Hanson. Mr. Davis and Herbert attended the same college. Mr. Davis remembered his old friend expressing great distaste when he admitted to him he was a shifter, back when they were in school together. So you can imagine his concern when this person showed up in Nightshade claiming to be someone else."

"But I don't understand," I said, "If the city council knew that Duke—I mean, Herbert—was a bad guy, why didn't you expose his real identity and pull him out of school?"

"Well, we didn't know for sure that he was the killer," Bianca admitted. "Not until now. But we thought that until we had proof, it would be best to keep him under observance. And what better way to do that than to allow him to remain in high school, with Penny Edwards keeping an eye on him at home?"

Bianca winked at me. I wondered if there was more to Penny than I had previously thought.

"I can't believe he hated paranormals so much that he

joined the Scourge," I said, shaking my head in disbelief. "How could anyone be so cruel and narrow-minded?"

"Unfortunately, paranormals are in more danger from his kind than you might think," Bianca said. "That's why we have to look out for each other. My assignment was to watch after you, Daisy." She smiled.

"But I'm not part of the paranormal community," I said. "Why would I need a guardian from the Scourge? Why would they want to kill me?"

"We don't think he was trying to kill you, Daisy," Bianca said. "We think he was trying to recruit you."

I shivered, then smiled at Bianca. "Lucky for me you're good at your job."

CHAPTER TWENTY-FOUR

The rest of the night was a blur of noise and excitement. Chief Mendez, who I now realized was a Were and a member of the Nightshade City Council—like father, like son—managed to hustle Duke out of the Wilder mansion without many people noticing.

Ryan, of course, noticed my long absence, so we found a quiet corner where I could tell him the whole thing.

He paled. "Daisy, you should have told me. You could have been killed."

"There was no time," I said. "But I promise I'll try to find you next time."

He put his head in his hands. "*Next* time? I don't think I'll survive."

I kissed him and pulled him to his feet. "C'mon, this is our prom. It's time to dance."

I danced until my new high heels gave me blisters and I was dying of thirst. I finally collapsed at the table, and Ryan went to get me a glass of punch.

"Ready to head to the after party?" Samantha asked me.

"Honestly?" I said. "I'm ready to crawl into bed."

"You can't!" she said. "We still have the after party and then breakfast at Slim's. If you don't show up, you know it'll freak your mom out."

I groaned. I'd forgotten Mom was volunteering at the cupcake booth at the party. "You're right," I said. "She'll probably think that Ryan and I snuck off somewhere or something."

"Were you going to?" Sam said curiously. "Because I can cover for you, if that's what you had in mind."

"No!" I said. "We just got back together. That's definitely *not* what I had in mind."

"What's not what you had in mind?" Ryan asked. He handed me a glass of punch, which I drank gratefully.

"Another dance," I improvised. "I'm ready to head to the party. What about you?"

"Sure," he said easily.

I ignored Sam, who was smothering a laugh behind her hand.

The limo was waiting outside, and it took us to the park, where the Dark Carnival was set up. When we passed by Samantha's old house, Sean put his arm around her and she put her head on his shoulder. I was pretty sure we wouldn't see Poppy at the after party, and I was right. She didn't show. And who could blame her?

It was a good thing that the park was so huge, because it

seemed as though everyone in Nightshade was there. Suddenly, I wasn't tired after all. The place looked perfect—perfectly creepy—with merry-go-round music playing on the loud-speaker and red lights strung up everywhere. Everyone kept telling me how great the park looked, and how much fun the party was. I was walking on air. The only thing that put a damper on the party was the dark, empty booth with a sign that read FORTUNES $1 where Duke Sherrad would have been.

But I passed by the booth a little while later, and there was Penny Edwards. She pointed to a copy of *A Goof-Ball's Guide to Fortune-Telling* and winked at me.

Two hours later I was bone tired, but I wasn't ready for the night to end. A bunch of us headed to Slim's for breakfast, so I called Rose to see if she and Poppy wanted to come.

"I'll ask," she said, "but don't count on it."

I turned to Ryan, who hadn't left my side since he'd heard about Duke. "It's a definite maybe."

Flo was working the morning shift and even gave us a grudging smile when she saw us in our prom finery.

She took our orders and then set down a pot of coffee and cups. I'm not sure that coffee was the best idea, since I planned to collapse in my bed right after breakfast, but it smelled so good I couldn't resist.

Nicholas and Rose showed up a few minutes later with Poppy in tow. She'd changed into jeans and a top. She was smiling, though it was a little droopy. Her eyes and nose were red, but she seemed okay.

All anyone could talk about was Duke.

"How did he do it?" Poppy asked.

"Remember those bushes we saw in the front of the house? Those are oleander bushes. He slipped oleander into Mr. Davis's tea," I said. "But he must have moved the body to the park to make it look like Mr. Davis had been attacked by a werewolf while he was jogging."

"What a horrible man," Rose said.

"And Mom kept seeing a cup. At least now we know how he was killed. And who did it," Poppy said.

"Rose, the day we were at his cottage, you said there was a piece missing from the set of china. Do you remember which one?"

She thought about it for a minute. "It was a teacup, I'm pretty sure."

"It's missing because Duke used it to poison Mr. Davis. He had to get rid of the evidence."

Conversation stopped when Flo came over, gave Poppy a hug, and whispered something in her ear. Flo never hugged anyone.

Ryan smiled at her. "I like your T-shirt," he said.

Flo positively glowed. She definitely had a soft spot for Ryan, but then again, who could blame her?

I took a closer look at her shirt. This one read, "keep night-shade weird."

I agreed.

As I watched Flo and Poppy, my gaze collided with Elise's. Her eyes glowed a terrible orange. She'd heard us talking about who killed her cousin, all right. She said something to Bane, and then he threw a couple of twenties on the table and they hurried out.

"The Wilder family are all shifters, right?" I said in a low voice. "Why didn't Mr. Davis just shift when Duke attacked him?"

"Mr. Davis was a shifter, all right, but it wouldn't have done him much good. He shifted to a rabbit," Nicholas said. "Which made it interesting at family reunions, since the rest of the Wilder pack are hunters."

"What happens to Duke—I mean, Herbert—now?" Ryan asked.

"The Nightshade City Council will deal with him," Nicholas said.

I had a strange feeling, from the look I had seen in Elise's eyes, that Duke would be dealt with very shortly. "Or the Wilder family will," I said. "Either way, he probably won't make it to trial." I felt a twinge of pity at the thought of what would happen to Duke if Elise caught up with him.

If Elise didn't get to him first, the Nightshade City Council would do whatever it took to guard the city's secrets from the Scourge, or anybody else.

Nightshade was full of secrets. I glanced at Ryan, who put his arms around me.

"Ready to go?" he asked. I smiled and nodded, but part of me was wondering what other secrets Nightshade held. I'd let the town keep its secrets for now, but somehow I knew that there was a big secret still hidden, a secret that could change my life.

Acknowledgments

I'd like to thank my two favorite high school teachers, Ms. Raymond and Mr. Wagner, for being fantastic, inspiring people who made my high school years not only bearable but intellectually stimulating. Thanks to my online writers groups yawriters and yanovelists for their support and wisdom. And to my family for not locking me out of the house when I'm on deadline.

Marlene Perez is the author of *Dead Is the New Black*, *Love in the Corner Pocket*, and *Unexpected Development*, which was named an ALA Quick Pick for Reluctant Young Adult Readers. She lives in Orange County, California, where she makes predictions based on her iTunes playlist. She's still searching for a prophetic jukebox.

www.marleneperez.com